Papa
Sartre

Papa
Sartre

Ali Bader

Translated by
Aida Bamia

The American University in Cairo Press
Cairo New York

First published in 2009 by
The American University in Cairo Press
113 Sharia Kasr el Aini, Cairo, Egypt
420 Fifth Avenue, New York, NY 10018
www.aucpress.com

Dar el Kutub No. 4131/09
ISBN 978 977 416 298 5

Dar el Kutub Cataloging-in-Publication Data

Bader, Ali
         Papa Sartre / Ali Bader; translated by Aida Bamia.—Cairo: The
    American University in Cairo Press, 2009
             p.   cm.
         ISBN 978 977 416 298 5
         1. Arabic fiction   I. Bamia, Aida (trans.)   II. Title
         892.73

1 2 3 4 5 6 7 8   14 13 12 11 10 09

Designed by Adam el Sehemy
Printed in Egypt

The Research Trip

That wicked devil Hanna Yusif, the macabre-looking gravedigger, and his depraved friend—whom he refers to by the curious Biblical name of Nunu Behar—were the ones who convinced me to write the biography of an Iraqi philosopher, who lived in al-Sadriya district in the sixties.

In truth, those two charlatans were not lacking a love of philosophy, nor were they without enthusiasm and genius. They were, however, truly short on honor and relied without exception on depravity.

I met them last winter. I visited them in a modest house overlooking the cemetery at the church of Umm al-Mauna behind al-Saadun Park. An Iraqi merchant who called himself Sadeq Zadeh—half mad, wanton, and entirely dishonest—had rented the room for them. I later learned he was the man financing the biography of the dead philosopher.

A friend working at the old manuscript library in Baghdad introduced me to them. I was mesmerized by Hanna's broken voice, his high-pitched tone, and his gravedigger's face. I met them on a cold, sunny December day. Hanna said to me with a certain visionary look while his hand rested on his girlfriend's shoulder—she never stopped chewing gum—"My house is in al-Saadun Park, near the Assyrian's grocery. I'll wait for you there on Sunday morning."

That Sunday I walked around the post office building, heading toward the Christian neighborhood that surrounds al-Saadun Park. Trees lined the street that ran between rows of one-story houses. I suddenly smelled the shiny rain-wet asphalt and spotted the Assyrian's grocery at the end of the main street. It wasn't a large store but a narrow shop really, with two wooden doors. There were two metal-leaf panels at the center, and the front of the grocery was covered with white tiles. Inside there was a marble stand filled with copper utensils and baskets of washed fruit; there were also bottles of whiskey, local arrack, and first-rate wine, all lined up neatly in the glass showcase. A photograph of a stiff figure wearing an embroidered and medal-bedecked costume was hanging on the wall behind the Assyrian. I asked him about Father Hanna's house. "Who told you he's a father?" he retorted, and burst out laughing. His white mustache stretched over his upper lip like milk, his blue eyes sank into their sockets, and his bony face seemed to mock me. It was his wife who replied, pointing a thin finger at a large green tree in the middle of the square, "There it is." In the only memory I have of her she is wearing her braids curled on top her head like a halo, medical glasses, and a sad countenance reminiscent of Eve's face after she was thrown out of Paradise. When I reached the cemetery fence, I saw a little house attached to a crumbling church. Water was running in a shallow creek along the fence, casting a silvery film in the air. I could hear the water flowing smoothly. I had to press up against the red brick wall to pass. The wall surrounded a rather large piece of land with a soft lawn and groups of roses that were planted without pattern; large trellises swayed under the impact of the birds jumping from corner to corner.

A man wearing drab trousers and a white scarf on his head, with a sharp knife in hand, was slaughtering a colorful rooster in the garden. He cut its throat and threw the creature onto the lawn, where it struggled in a pool of blood. I asked him if this was Hanna Yusif's house. He said yes. A drop of red blood on the lawn shone in the glare of the sun.

Our encounter was warm and friendly. Hanna smiled constantly, making his small mustache look like a trace of red wine. He led me to the living room. The curtains on the windows were embroidered with small pink flowers. I could hear the shower running and a car's tires squealing on the asphalt road.

I asked him if someone else was home, and he said, "Nunu is in the shower." I asked him again about the philosopher and the books he had published during his lifetime. He shook his small red head with his shining blue eyes, "No, none at all. This presumptuous fellow did not write a single book in his whole life."

"Presumptuous?" I said, surprised.

"Every philosopher is presumptuous," said Nunu Behar as she walked past us, naked, coming out of the bathroom.

"I don't understand," I said, staring at Nunu Behar, who was standing in front of a sofa covered with silk cushions. She buttoned her shirt and put on her pants without underwear. She left the top button unbuttoned and looked straight at me. I could see her ample breasts under the soft fabric of the shirt. She continued, "Yes! Every philosopher is presumptuous, but there are those who write books and make their biographer's job easy and others who don't write books and force us to pay someone to dig for information, lie, and make things up to make true philosophers out of them."

Her style of speech surprised me. She seemed to believe that writing a philosopher's biography was an easy undertaking. She had sensed that I was apprehensive about writing this one, which would explain her indirectly trying to dissuade me from not doing so.

Her face was dripping with water and her jet-black hair shone under the light of the corner lamp. When she reached me she said, "You know, a philosopher is a fabrication, it is true . . . believe me, a fabrication." I could sense the heat of her skin under the open shirt that revealed her generous breasts. I asked her, "Who creates this fabrication?" The two scoundrels said in unison, "We do." Then Hanna added, "You will write this man's biography and we'll cover your expenses for collecting information and documents and then we'll pay you for writing." Nunu added, "Today we'll give you some papers and some geographical pointers for you to get started with. But please, don't think that this is going to be a difficult project. His life was simple, extremely simple."

"Do you think so?" I said. She replied, "I do."

I was truly happy with the promised sum of money, especially because I was totally penniless. Only my friend, the investigator in the manuscript library, knew how broke I was. But when those two scoundrels saw my joy at the prospect of a handsome sum of money and my willingness to undertake the project, they probably sensed my desperation. They immediately gathered the various papers, large folders, and documents that were scattered in their study. Hanna handled the red leather books roughly, pushing aside large glass inkwells on a desk with all sorts of colored pens, pins, and quills and a smaller inkwell with red ink. He explained, "These are important documents that will acquaint you with the philosopher's childhood, his school years, and the people who used to know him."

Hanna took a handkerchief from the pocket of his plaid trousers, with which he wiped off the desk, and sat on a rattan chair. He looked at me surreptitiously, handed me a thick striped file, and said, "This is Nadia Khaddouri's family file. They were partners with the Lawi family, the car dealers." He then took out another pile of square sheets and said, "These are important papers. They concern Shaul."

Nunu Behar added, "These documents and data aren't really enough. They'll only show you where to start and where to find more information and important papers." She was chewing gum while she spoke, and her eyes projected an exciting glitter of desire. I turned my gaze toward the papers in my hand and began to examine them. They weren't documents in the real sense of the word but rather little snippets of information written in a vulgar and gushing style. Some were no more than encomiums written by those who had otherwise considered the philosopher stupid during his lifetime. Others, in a most sycophantic way, attested to his wisdom and genius. These papers wouldn't be a real source of information but could be important because they shed light on some of the preliminary problems related to the biography. Clearly, the real problem with these papers was that they consisted of piles of highly indigestible materials, written in a vulgar style, boringly flattering, and wholly lacking in impartiality. What I was looking for was a document that would contain objective information. At this point even a dull document would provide a great deal of help.

The documents Hanna handed me were written in an affected and biased style. Throughout the period of my work on the biography, frankly, they were more of a handicap than a help. I tried to liven them up with irony and made fun of their repellent nature and superficiality. Page after page, I had to deal with fables such as "No sooner did the philosopher touch the branch standing before Husniya than its flowers bloomed," or "No sooner did he take the chicken in his arms than it laid an egg weighing half a kilogram in his lap."

I was going over documents that could turn a carriage conductor into a silent, huge, mysterious giant. They revealed the ability of some people to distort, imitate, and contradict without being aware how much their gibberish defied reason. More important for me were the names, an abundance of names: names of servants, masters, men of letters, merchants, children, and renowned personalities. Obviously I'd have to look for them elsewhere, and not in those documents written in such a repulsive and provocative style.

I asked Hanna if the philosopher had had friends, but it was Nunu Behar who replied in her lazy tone, "We'll introduce you to the merchant Sadeq Zadeh. He's the only one who knows a great deal about his private life. There is also Butrus Samhiri the lawyer. You must meet him as well. He has official documents that will help you with your project."

We sat around the marble fireplace on chairs with green satin cushions. A weak light came from the darkness of the chimney, and when Nunu Behar opened the window I immediately smelled the scent of her breasts mixed with a hint of earth and the lingering traces of strong perfume.

"When will you start working?" asked Hanna Yusif.

"Tomorrow," I said.

"I'll write letters of recommendation. They might help facilitate your mission. I have a piece of advice for you as well."

"What is it?" Nunu Behar was playing with a chain that rested between her breasts. "Are you a moral person?" he asked, smiling.

"I am an honest man," I said immediately.

"You must be weary of that," they both said and laughed in a quiet, subdued manner. Nunu Behar moved away from me with her wild hair, raising her hand and revealing a small expanse of skin between her underarm and breast.

"We're not paying you because you're an honest man. No, not at all," said Nunu Behar. She broke into soft laugher, then carried on in a lazy voice, "We are all honest, but honesty does not put bread on the table."

"I don't understand," I said to Hanna, "do you want me to tell the truth or falsify it?"

"It's something else," he said, adding, "You must know that truth and bogus facts are not necessarily a contradiction in your kind of work. Anyway, you're not being paid to write a true story."

"I'll write about his greatness and his commonness at the same time," I explained.

"Write whatever you want, and make this donkey greater than Sartre himself. I couldn't care less. You and I can decide on the important details of his life," said Hanna

Nunu clarified, "When you reach the conclusion you will understand."

Frankly, I didn't understand much of what they said, but I quickly realized that working with these two scoundrels wouldn't be easy. They had other demands that I found difficult to accept. After a few minutes of silence I realized that I should leave. I excused myself and promised to see them again in a few days.

Hanna came to me and took my hand as if to escort me out in a tender and sincerely affectionate manner. Nunu Behar was sitting on a rattan chair directly behind him. She had put her legs up on a marble stool covered with a white embroidered silk tablecloth, her knees parted in a relaxed and provocative manner.

It was almost noon when I left their house. I wandered the narrow streets of al-Saadun Park and observed the wet sidewalks and the pillars supporting the buildings. I noticed they were made of coarse bricks. I saw young women enter the church, dressed in finely woven western clothes and high heels, their heads covered with light, filigree veils. Bells were tolling. Their metallic ringing echoed between the houses of the neighborhood.

I hadn't met Hanna Yusif or Nunu Behar before, but I realized that those two had intentions that went beyond commissioning the mere writing of the biography—in other words, something in the story that went beyond the biography itself. It was one of those things that one ignores for various reasons, and my reason was my desperate need for money. I was so destitute I couldn't hesitate or object. I had to act quickly and think later. I admit that mine was not a very moral attitude, but I never had been obsessively moral in my life—nor an enthusiastic scandal-seeker—but I never knew that honor and moral conduct could have such a poisonous impact on some people.

I wasn't at all concerned by the need to achieve a moral *chef d'œuvre,* but I didn't want to create the kind of distortion proposed by Hanna Yusif and Nunu Behar either. I wasn't obsessed with goodness, nobility, chastity, or rigor. I didn't want to make the biography an expression of awe or exaggerated admiration or enmity, as those two scoundrels would have me do. I was not devoid of violent feelings or the capacity to fabricate facts like any other person, but I was unwilling to delve into the tragic history of the world. I had always been filled with a sense of freedom, and my morality had not been corrupted by my feelings of love or hatred.

The following day I examined the documents, photographs, papers, and other information Hanna and Nunu Behar had given me. I must admit, however, that I didn't expect the matter to be easy or transparent. I found the insolence and insults that filled the language those two scoundrels used with me amusing. They had also seduced me with their irresistible charm and their ability to belittle and crush people. They won me over with their games, in which they mixed truth with lies and exaggeration with forgery, seemingly without contradictions. They sometimes succeeded in making me notice an absence of diligence and conveying a need for me to exert leniency regarding objectivity.

I don't know why Nunu Behar fascinated me, whether it was her skills, her scandalous comportment, or her immorality. Maybe it was because she liberated me from something I had long despised in myself, a tendency to idealize and stand in awe of a personality who is now reduced to mere dust in a tomb.

On Tuesday morning we went out looking for information and documents related to the philosopher's life. A man called Jawad accompanied me. Hanna Yusif had chosen him to be my companion and watch my every move. Jawad's face resembled a pickpocket's: harsh wrinkled features, dark reddish skin, and a drooping mustache stained yellow from cigarettes. Jawad was hiding inside clothes that he was wearing for the first time and which did not fit him well. I was sure that Hanna had asked him to watch me rather than keep me company. This didn't bother me at all, and I tried my best to use him for my own purposes.

The late morning sun that day was pale, hidden by white scattered clouds, as we began to gather oral accounts and documents and take pictures of the district where the philosopher had lived in the sixties. I asked Jawad, who was carrying a camera on his chest, to choose the best angles to show the beauty and authentic character of al-Mahalleh, in particular the market, adjoining alleys, the mosque, the khan, the stable, and other sights. Then I prepared a detailed plan for describing the locations that the philosopher frequented to acquire background information that would help me define his personality.

Making our way through the dimly lit streets of al-Sadriya was difficult. They twisted and turned and then all ended in a vast avenue inaugurated by King Ghazi in the thirties. We tripped constantly on small damaged bumps, which blocked our way, difficult to see due to the many potholes full of water. These were deep enough to half cover the wheels of the small carts that crossed the alleys leading to the painters' market or Mahallet Siraj al-Din and the Shurja market. Every now and then we had to press against the humid walls of the houses to avoid the carts pulled by reddish large-rumped horses. Their muted whinnying pushed out of their nostrils like thick steam because of the cold air and the whips of coachmen, who shouted "careful, careful, and careful" to alert pedestrians.

I needed to draw a small map of Mahallet Siraj al-Din that would indicate the places where the philosopher had been. I recorded a detailed description of his vast house located at the top of Dr. Simon Bahlawan Boulevard. I gathered information as well about a stable located near Siraj al-Din Mosque. The stable was covered by a sturdy trellis, piles of hay, and used cartwheels. There was also a khan close to the stable. The guardian had been sleeping on the long bench in front of the café facing the mosque, getting ready for the night patrol. A water jar was in the middle of the open space. I located the Jewish merchant Shaul's shop in al-Sadriya souk. It was a small store that had changed aspect a thousand times since Shaul immigrated to London in the seventies. I had to draw a very precise map for the public transportation system that linked the house to the various locations frequented by the philosopher after he returned from Paris and achieved fame in Baghdad. There were also the locations that shaped his life and were relatively distant from Mahallet al-Sadriya. My first responsibility was to measure the distance between his house in al-Sadriya, where he lived with his French wife, and his grandfather's house, where he was born and spent his childhood and youth. It was located in al-Maarif Street, near the Greek Armenian Church. The next location was Nadia Khaddouri's house, an old building on the same street.

I had to establish the relation between these locations and the important personalities who played a role in the life of the philosopher. The list included Ismail Hadoub, who lived for a while in the fifties in the khan adjacent to Siraj al-Din Mosque. There was Shaul, the Lawi family, Nadia Khaddouri, who used to work in Mackenzie's bookshop on al-Rashid Street, and Edmond al-Qushli, who was nicknamed 'Trotsky' in the sixties. The philosopher met him at the Waqwaq café in Bab al-Muadham where he used to sit with people like Desmond Stewart and groups such as the sentries of al-Sadriya, One-Eyed Jaseb, Dalal Masabni the dancer, Rujina the maid, Husniya the washerwoman, Saadun the horse valet, Atiya the gardener, and others.

The research, mapping out of the important locations, and the identification of the places that influenced the philosopher's life took at least two months. I had to identify the public places where the philosopher was a frequent visitor, places such as the Grief Adab nightclub owned by Dalal Masabni, who had also been the philosopher's mistress for a time, and a group of other dancers who adopted his philosophy. There was also the Swiss café on al-Rashid Street, where the philosopher met regularly with literary figures, people such as Ismail Hadoub, Edmond al-Qushli, and others. I then moved to Orient Express café on al-Rashid Street, where the philosopher used to meet Nadia Khaddouri during his visits to Baghdad. He used to go to the Qadri al-Ardarumli cinema for the French movie evenings, to the Roxy cinema's foyer, where he met close family friends, and the Royal cinema's foyer. He also frequented Mackenzie's bookstore, where he bought the latest books on existentialism. Finally, I went to Nadi al-Alawiya, the club where he usually met his relatives, some childhood friends, and political figures who knew his father.

The more I learned about important aspects of the philosopher's life, the more entranced I became. I mean that I enjoyed the simple comments that shed light on an obscure or ambiguous period in his life, since I was well aware that gathering those remarks and reconstructing them to write the biography of a man now reduced to ashes was by no means an easy task. Every now and then I had to subject myself to a terrible process of deceit by people who would exaggerate every simple matter to give it importance, motivated by their ability to dramatize an ordinary event and surround it with a halo of sanctity.

I met people who admired all those who had departed us and would provide wondrous information, so distorted that it was impossible to trace their fantasies back to the original reality. I had to sift through this information, clean it, and keep track of the simple and temporary changes it underwent. When I met Rujina the maid, now an old, poor, and broken woman, who was shabbily dressed, she did not reveal the slightest information about the philosopher's childhood and teenage years. She looked beyond all his mistakes and stupidities and never admitted to any scandal. She elaborated on the magnanimity of his family and their honor, the great generosity of his parents, and their dignity and virtuousness. So I found myself gathering information that was heavy in virtue but light in vice. I needed to be constantly aware of my informants' linguistic tricks and examine closely their unlimited support and compassion for a man whom they despised during his lifetime and for whose tragic end they might possibly have been responsible.

I was given some letters and checks—information that did not lack a touch of caricature—but in hindsight I am convinced that the philosopher's personality was ultimately destroyed by liars who soft-pedaled certain matters, and by other people who in most instances exaggerated matters beyond what was acceptable and appropriate. While searching for information about his private life, I encountered his weaknesses and denials and his attachment to beliefs and ideas. They distorted his image and ended up giving him, in a complex way, distinctive traits that were much harsher than those he naturally possessed. I must admit that the information I received from Hanna Yusif and Nunu Behar was not so bad when stacked up against the conversations of the people who talked about him, the intellectuals who were his contemporaries, in particular. They spoke of him in an unfocused way, and even in a five- or six-hour interview they didn't provide much information at all.

I had met one of them on a Friday at the Saraya market as he sat squatting, looking for old books among the volumes spread out on the floor. I approached him and told him I'd like to get information about the philosopher. As soon as I spoke he stood up holding several books under his arm. He looked like a pasha's deputy: his black velvet headgear slightly bent, a straight mustache that looked like a ribbon with straight edges, his vest buttoned snugly over his round belly. He stood up straight, facing me and standing among books that were spread all over the floor. It was a comical scene of a man standing in the middle of a crowd, jostled to left and right, his voice mixed with the shouts of the papermakers, booksellers, and the horns of the cars in the narrow, crowded street.

He replied with a lengthy narrative, "The late philosopher was a great man; he married Sartre's cousin. He taught the sixties generation about the absurd and about nausea. Suhail Idris, the existentialist of the time, had great admiration for the philosopher. It was an important philosophy in our time. All this is gone now, unfortunately, and our generation was the only one that read *Les chemins de la liberté* (The Roads to Freedom), *La nausée* (Nausea), and *L'être et le néant* (Being and Nothingness). Our nihilism was real. It wasn't phony. We fought the spies and the collaborators because we were aware of the essence of existence."

Every time I put my finger on something, he eluded it. I had the impression I was trying to get hold of an imaginary bottle, a mirage. Though it might be difficult for me to remember those ideas and images, which have disappeared for good, it was very hard for me, as I listened to the words of his contemporaries, to find any truth in them. There was nothing but the remnants of dust. I am almost convinced that those stupid guys were truly crazy.

It was incumbent upon me to collect everything; I went after anything I could get. I gathered documents from everybody, whether they contained insults or praise, from common gardeners, uncouth citizens, flattering hypocrites, frivolous men, noble servants, politicians, and saints. Using my intuition I would sketch the background of each based on their names and manners, and then interpret them. Later I would study the feelings stirred up in evoking the memory of the philosopher. I benefited from the documents that Hanna Yusif gave me, especially the documents with narratives, the memoirs, and the photographs and diaries of the philosopher, his father, and others. I eliminated the documents containing comments, which were nothing more than directives inserted by Hanna Yusif and Nunu Behar meant to distort facts and mislead me. They were vulgar and filled with lies and were easy to identify because they were written in a different hand and with various pens. Though they did not contradict the documents I found in other places, I excluded them because they were a contemporary interpretation of past events. I finally realized that the truly important papers were in the hands of two individuals. One was the lawyer Butrus Samhiri, who was in possession of official documents that traced the key episodes in the philosopher's life and which contained important details. I had to reconstitute them in order to provide a clear image of the philosopher's public life. The other person was the merchant Sadeq Zadeh, an Iraqi who traded in art objects, carpets, and antiques. The documents in his possession covered an important period in the life of the philosopher, his thinking, and his secret relationships with dancers, prostitutes, and public figures. Those would help me depict the inner feelings of the philosopher, his intimate life, and his psychological profile.

I went to see Butrus Samhiri late one morning accompanied by Jawad. His office was located in Ras al-Qaryeh on the top floor of a building at the entrance to the quarter, on al-Rashid Street. Jawad looked funny, with a camera hanging around his neck and a straw summer hat tilted to one side on his head. I could not help laughing at the sight, but he responded to my laughter with a smile that seemed to say that he was feeling important for the first time in his life, or that he was proud to be undertaking an important task. I smiled back at him. I walked beside him, without looking at him, and asked, "What were you doing before working with me, Jawad?"

"I worked with my uncle Hanna," he replied, keeping pace, his back slightly bent.

"What exactly did you do with your uncle Hanna?" I inquired as we crossed the bridge heading toward al-Mustansir Street. Jawad said, "He trusted me to do everything." We busied ourselves looking at the jewelry shops. We saw Sabian jewelers in long gray beards holding torches with strong flames to gold rings with precious stones. There were also shops selling watches, perfumes, western clothes, and quality shoes. We took a slight turn down a narrow street toward a building with a faded red tile roof from which water dripped onto the bars of the upper windows. A huge pomegranate tree grew in the middle of the sidewalk. Its branches had damaged the telephone lines. This alley was given the name al-Adliya Street in the forties because of the large number of attorneys who had their offices in the surrounding buildings. A very tall policeman with a wide leather belt stood rigidly on the corner. His trousers were tight and pegged to the cuffs. He wore a revolver on his left side, and he held a thick billy club made of striped walnut. He stared straight ahead. When Jawad spied him from a distance he stopped short, his thick neck sinking between his shoulders, his arms and legs shaking. He opened his mouth so wide that I could see all his crooked back teeth. His eyes turned red and he breathed with difficulty. I was so surprised by his alarm that I couldn't help but confront him, asking in a low voice, "Jawad, Jawad, what happened to you? Are you afraid of the policeman?"

"Yes, yes," he said, hiding behind me like someone ready to bolt. I held him firmly by the hand and asked, "Why, Jawad? Have you done something wrong?"

"No, but I deserted the army." His mustache was shaking, and he tried to lower his hat over his face as we passed the policeman, who didn't pay any attention to us but continued to look straight ahead. We entered the vast hall of the building, where a servant was holding a bucket and mopping the marble stairs. We asked where the attorney Butrus Samhiri's office was, and he pointed one flight up When we reached the second floor we saw the lawyer's nameplate before us. The office door was wide open.

The strong odor of whiskey wafted lazily through the open door. An old gramophone sat atop a square box on a dark wooden commode with elaborate old Indian designs. Old black records were piled on top of each other in an attractive way, reaching the tip of the long-necked copper horn that extended from the record player.

We were met by a plump woman of moderate beauty, perhaps in her forties. She was calm in a sort of fatalistic manner. Her face was desiccated, her body was soft in a scandalous way, and her heavy breasts swung when she moved from one spot to another. She obviously excited Jawad, who was watching her fixedly and smiled at her with his wrinkled dark face and yellowed equine teeth.

"We came to see Mr. Butrus, the attorney," I said, bowing my head appropriately. "Do you have an appointment?" she asked. Her eyes moved from Jawad to me. "We do not have an appointment," I said, "but tell him that Hanna Yusif sent us." She smiled and welcomed us warmly. Her features changed, and it was clear that she knew Hanna Yusif very well—or at least the mere mention of the scoundrel's name erased any expression of fear.

She sat us down in the comfortable armchairs in the waiting room, went into the office, and, returning with her beautiful smile, escorted us to Mr. Butrus's office. She closed the door behind us, but Jawad could not take his eyes off the movement of her large hips. We sat facing a wall covered from top to bottom with yellow and red tiles. The other walls in the office were covered with thick mahogany panels. There was also a large, half-round balcony with colored marble at the edges. Butrus was sitting behind his desk and, due to his small size, only his head was visible. He jumped up from behind the desk to greet us, a thin, tiny man wearing a worn-out suit.

"Ahlan, Ahlan wa marhaba." He had a speech defect, mispronouncing his *r*s and mixing up some words. We sat in front of him, and he looked at us with sad eyes set in a stony face. He had a pencil behind his ear like a carpenter. I said, "I came for the documents," but he interrupted me and did not let me finish. "Yes, Hanna told me. All the documents are ready." He turned toward the library, which was filled with files, pushed some papers aside, and placed the documents on his tidy desk. They were simple: old official documents, bank checks, and photographs that had belonged to the philosopher and his family and friends. They included two photographs of him with his friend Nadia Khaddouri, one taken in Mackenzie's bookstore, and the other at the Orient Express café.

"Did you ever meet the philosopher?" I asked. He was staring at the half-open door of a small room from which the strong whiskey smell emanated. "Yes, I used to be his father's agent, may his soul rest in peace. He belonged to an aristocratic family, and although the revolution brought them down, it didn't change their standards. But Abd al-Rahman revolted against his family, even before the revolution."

"Did you know him well?" I asked. Butrus Samhiri stared at me with a piercing look.

"Yes I did, I did. I met him more than once, but those were casual encounters. We never discussed serious topics when we met, and as a result we did not really connect." He was silent for a moment, then continued as if he had just remembered, "I was a minor employee, a clerk, as they say. Existentialism was meaningless to me. I was more inclined toward the left, and I found Edmond al-Qushli, the Trotskyite of our time, more to my liking than the philosopher of al-Sadriya. I was not able to understand Sartre's complicated philosophy, and I didn't like him."

"Did you find his philosophy complicated?" I asked.

"I don't think that anyone in my generation understood the things he used to read. Those who said they did are liars. You can ask Salman and Abbas, if you wish. He used to meet with them in the Café Brazil."

"But could you understand Trotsky?" I asked. Jawad was trying to take a picture, but I dissuaded him.

"Trotskyism is not a philosophy the way existentialism is. It has a practical side." He felt uncomfortable now, and it was clear that he didn't want to go on. He stood up and handed me the documents. "Examine these papers and if you need anything else contact me."

I stood up. So did Jawad, who, burdened by the camera hanging around his neck, almost tripped and fell onto the sofa. "Where can I find Abbas and Salman?" I asked.

"You'll find them in al-Camp market. Ask around; everybody there knows them. Just ask for Abbas Philosophy; they'll direct you to them." He turned to Jawad and asked, "Hey, Jawad, do you still catch birds on people's roofs?" Jawad blushed and laughed maliciously. I asked Butrus how he knew Jawad.

"I know him because Hanna asked me to represent him in a few cases." He laughed loudly, shaking his head like a devil. We left and immediately headed for the Adhamiya quarter to meet two of the philosopher's old friends who had become merchants in Camp Raghiba Khatun market.

Jawad hurried along behind me, his eyes deep in their sockets. The weather was refreshingly humid. The cool air hit my face, and the sun was warm, especially when we walked on the bright side of the street. We were walking on al-Rashid Street, where the many groceries displayed boxes of toffee, sweets, and all kinds of confections. Boutiques, tailor shops, watch shops, and jewelry stores lined the street, and people crowded into the restaurants for cheap sandwiches.

I was thinking about the philosopher's companions from the sixties who had turned to selling fruit at al-Camp market after becoming involved in philosophy. I had to see them, to get something from them that I could use—or at least obtain their photographs to include in the book. We walked toward the square and caught a taxi after Jawad bought a pack of cigarettes and lit one up. We arrived as the clock of al-Imam al-A'dham was on its third ring. The place was crowded with buyers and salesmen. In the fruit market we inquired about the two men and were told that they were in the restaurant at the end of the main street.

The market was humid and stuffy, the ground was muddy, and water seeped from the badly paved street. The restaurant was located at one end of the market, a small place with a low ceiling, painted a cheap white and with a dirty glass facade. All kinds of people pressed together inside—fruit and spice merchants wearing their white dishdashas with belts tied around plump bellies, young men wearing western clothes, policemen in khaki uniforms and boots, their thick walnut billy clubs on the table, and women in black abayas. A large grill at the entrance of the restaurant filled the air with the smell of coal and grilled meat. The servers were rushing about, wearing white aprons and caps bearing the restaurant's name. We were greeted by the sounds of orders being shouted across the restaurant—kebab, salad without vinegar, bread—the metallic sound of spoons and plates dropped onto the sticky tables, and the clamor of the dishwashers echoing on the wet brick floor.

We inquired about Abbas Philosophy and Salman. They didn't look like philosophers at all, more like fruit merchants. They were middle-aged men with huge bellies that hit the edge of the table whenever they moved. Their table was filled with all kinds of grilled meat, bread, pickles, grilled onions, and vegetables. They welcomed me and Jawad very warmly and were extremely surprised to learn that someone, finally, had remembered them. One of them said, "You've finally remembered the great men of the country. We were afraid to die for fear that our memory and that of the greatest Arab philosopher, the philosopher of al-Sadriya, would be lost forever."

They talked and ate while I looked over their fat faces and the new outfits they wore, with narrow ties and starched collars, a style that was popular in the sixties. They talked with their mouths full, round, bald heads covered with sweat, and glasses continuously slipping off their noses. When their mouths were too full they would push the food in with their fingers. They took turns talking about the philosopher, while I took notes and Jawad ate—he dug in as soon as they invited us to join them. I reproached him and kicked him in the foot, but he ignored me and kept on eating. He shared their food, making sandwiches of kebab and grilled onions. A piece of celery fell out of his mouth onto the table.

They talked like all those I'd talked to already. I searched for words that would put me on the right path, but to no avail. They embellished the philosopher's image with made-up stories as if decorating a Christmas tree with random shiny and colorful baubles. They meant well, yet what they gave me were falsifications, perhaps prompted by a desire to hide their embarrassment at having been so long ignored and estranged. They provided me with their information and histrionic comments, played roles, and incongruously arrogated importance to themselves, sometimes obviously, but usually more subtly.

Their comments about the sixties sounded more like crying over a lost Eden that had cast out the philosopher. Nonetheless, I had no choice but to write down everything, both the noble and heroic motivations that I mutely condemn and the ignoble and sordid emotions that I respect. Such feelings prove that the philosopher was a human being, not a legendary hero, that he was weak, mean, and lazy like the rest of us, not a god.

Sitting face to face with these two I felt I was dealing with people who organize their lives into a tight system, believing it to be full and complete, the only life worth living. I'm tempted to say that they can't conceive of the existence of the lives of others who preceded them or others that followed. They're unable to view things except through their own glasses, lenses of their own making. The men ate nonstop, leaving me little time for questions. No sooner would one stop than the other would start up. I felt squeezed between them. They imparted both valuable and insignificant information, critical and ordinary remarks, and they kept insisting that I consider everything they were saying very important. I thus found myself writing down mostly what they wanted me to record and not much of what I wanted.

What I was really looking for was the thread that would lead me to the root of the matter. I was seeking highly germane testimonies from people whom I expected to be gifted or endowed with more refined vision than the average person and who could provide me with valuable information that would eliminate the possibility of distortion.

These two men were not distinct from ordinary people in their view of the philosopher. Their representation of the philosopher was the same I encountered everywhere: among his friends he was seen as an amalgam of virtues, and his enemies saw him as an amalgam of vices. Theirs was first and foremost a moral evaluation. They'd say, "He is the Sartre of the Arab World, and Sartre sent him to save the nation and put an end to the life of banditry brought about by the fifties. His life was complete and pure, a model of greatness and beauty because he did not begin it, as others did, with serious weaknesses."

I left the low-ceilinged restaurant with Jawad, who felt happy and satiated, having eaten his fill. A dog loitered outside, drinking water, and two wet cats waited for leftover kebab. Jawad took a photograph as they were eating and was pleased with himself. He smoked a cigarette and blew the smoke from his nose and mouth into the cold air.

The clouds were getting thicker, and the winter evening sun was sinking behind the minaret. The blue of the sky and the white clouds were tinted with a trace of red. We walked until we reached the royal cemetery with its wet, dark green trees. A patch of red sun covered their tops. It gradually got colder, and walking was becoming difficult. Our fingers were freezing, our faces were turning red, and our limbs trembled from cold. We each took a taxi, Jawad to Hanna Yusif's house, and I to my apartment.

That evening I found myself facing thousands of documents, photographs, scraps of information, and commentaries about the al-Sadriya philosopher. They all described an unusual personality, unique in its kind, a personality that represented both the dramatic world of a whole society and the tragic loneliness of an entire nation. It was my task to assess the destructive impact of the imaginary personality that had been catapulted to the rank of the gods, somehow bring this image down from the dizzying heights to which they had projected it in order to fill a huge gap in their own souls, and cope with the bitterness of their failed accomplishment.

No one among them understood his multifaceted character or the contradictions that produced his positive energy. Nor were they aware of the true nature of his humanity, a distinction of his rather than a defect. I was aware of his weaknesses as I laid the appropriate pieces of fabric to clothe his stripped body and each time I added a new feature to his face. I was searching under his diverse apparitions for the evolution of his personality, the pitches of his wellbeing, and his feelings as they interconnected with those of the world that surrounded him. I was trying to find the rhythm of his childhood and youth and his relationships within the huge social complex. I would not have been able to accept his great value before I had found in it all kinds of meanness, lowness, and vileness, which I considered to be true manifestations of human nature.

I was not able to trace the outlines of the philosopher's external appearance and physical form before imposing on his existence a semblance of unity within the order that produced it. In other words, I was looking for the system that provided him with this kind of support, one that exhausted and worried him, in which stupidity played the role of self-effacement, concern with people's happiness, and a desire for organized reform. Because of my inability—for various reasons—to put all this material into one mold, I had to believe in him and in his philosophy and search for everything: the flowers he loved, the food he ate, the basin in which he washed, the smell of his soap lingering on the wood of the slippery floor. I had to describe his love for gardens, depict his impressions, and examine my own emotions toward those things. I had to look for a series of unusual events that elicited those feelings and moved him as a philosopher. I needed to find his happy, peaceful memories, his love stories—all those anxious feelings connected to events lost in a sea of obscurity.

At that time I could not find a single person who had retained a genuine memory of him, not one recollection untarnished by forgetfulness that contained a charming image of him. I needed one to place in the appropriate social frame, in its intellectual venue, and in its appropriate location in the biography. Overcome by confusion and distress, I spent hours searching for information. Nadia Khaddouri had disappeared and did not leave a forwarding address, and so had Ismail Hadoub. There were conflicting stories about the philosopher's disappearance. His French wife had returned to Paris, his father had died, and despite repeated promises by Hanna Yusif to introduce his children to me, I never met them. The only person I was able to meet was Sadeq Zadeh, thanks to Hanna Yusif, who arranged the appointment with him.

I was walking alone that afternoon, toward a high palace behind the railway station. I had to cross a farm growing lettuce and red radishes. I watched the dark bony-faced peasants working, moving swiftly in the mud and straw near Nadhem Pasha's small bridge. I could hear the sound of the horses' hooves on the pavement of the main street, mixed with other sounds. The palace had high balconies, and its upper floors were covered with beautiful tiles. Sloughi dogs were barking in the garden.

A servant dressed in a colorful Lebanese costume received me. His face was covered with freckles, he had a bushy mustache, and he wore a small cap. He led me to the expensive metal main gate, rang the bell beside the door, and adjusted a thick silver watch that he pulled out of his pants pocket. We walked through a foyer with a polished white marble floor and into a large hall. Black marble stairs led to the second floor. The railing was made of wood and stone and overlooked the inner hall.

I was totally surprised to see Nunu Behar come out of the parlor on the right, while Sadeq Zadeh appeared at the top of the stairs, looking extremely elegant. As he walked down the marble stairs the light from the lamp on the table illuminated his beautiful trousers and the marvelous colors of his necktie. Nunu Behar greeted me with her warm fleshy hand and looked at me with her round face and her slightly full figure. The three of us sat in a room inlaid with precious stones and decorations. A high balcony overlooked rubber trees with dark green leaves. She said to me in a soft, lazy voice, "This is Sadeq Zadeh. You must cooperate with him," to which I replied, "But I came especially to seek his cooperation."

The place had an ambiance of intimacy. Sadeq Zadeh smiled at me with his handsome face and graying hair, while his malicious eyes darted nervously. He explained his position, "Yes, I will cooperate with you, but for my own sake and not for Hanna Yusif." At this moment I looked at Nunu Behar, whose long black hair fell onto her shoulders. Her sensual face smiled at me. I could feel her humid skin under her thick woolen sweater. "You work for Sadeq Zadeh, not Hanna Yusif," she explained. "What about you?" I asked, hardly hiding my surprise. "I'm with Sadeq, of course. What do you think? He is the only one financing the project. Do you think bankrupt Hanna is the one with the money?" I continued, "You didn't say that before."

"Everything in due time," she explained.

"Why didn't Sadeq Zadeh contact me first?" I asked.

"This matter does not concern you," said Sadeq Zadeh, who seemed slightly upset. He added, "Look at all these files, they're yours. They are the files of his true biography. This is what you're looking for. I have them, not Hanna. You should only be concerned with the money and the files, and both are with me, naturally. I'll provide you with everything, and we'll end the project together. You'll finish it up with me, not with Hanna."

"I'll do that, but what if Hanna asks me for the conclusion ending the work?" I asked. "Nunu and I will work things out," he explained. "But I'm obligated to share the conclusion with him, since he is the one providing me with the money," I replied, slightly upset. "It is Nunu's money, and Nunu works with me, not with Hanna," explained Sadeq.

"Why this insistence on the conclusion of the finished work?" I asked. When he heard my question, the expression on his face changed. He was smiling and so was Nunu, who was looking at him. He left his desk, brought two glasses of whiskey, and asked if I cared for a drink. Upon my negative reply, he gave the glass to Nunu and explained, "In reality there are things that do not concern you as you write. I won't prevent you from writing the truth, not at all. I won't ask you to write things that are not mentioned in the documents. The problem, however, is with the philosopher's death. People don't agree on the circumstances of his death. There are many versions. All I want is to choose one of the various endings and ask you to adopt it. I don't want to do what Hanna is doing, which is to involve you. All I want is for you to present me with all the plausible endings, and I'll choose the one I want."

As a matter of fact I was very pleased with this meeting, since making such a choice would be inescapable. And we might even agree on the same ending. If one of the versions were acceptable and then adopted, I wouldn't mind choosing it. I took the documents and left the house.

That evening I began writing the first words of the biography of the existentialist Iraqi philosopher nicknamed the Sartre of al-Sadriya.

The Writing Journey

1

The big clock in al-Sadriya souk chimed seven, waking Abd al-Rahman from his sleep. The sound was mixed with the shouting of street merchants selling vegetables, poultry, and fresh fruits, while the butchers, bakers, and fighting beggars gathered at the entrance of the souk. He was feeling sick. He slowly got out of bed and looked at a photograph of Jean-Paul Sartre hanging on the wall facing him. It was a gray photograph in a beautiful golden frame hung above shelves holding a selection of philosophy books, prominent among them were the French editions of Sartre's books, organized carefully by title and content—*L'être et le néant, Le Mur, L'existentialisme est un humanisme, Les chemins de la liberté, Les mouches*—and some volumes of the journal *Les temps modernes*.

Abd al-Rahman's house was located at the far end of Dr. Simon Bahlawan Boulevard, overlooking the open section of the aluminum-roofed souk. It was an extremely tidy house, elegant and beautiful. The rugs were thick Kashani, the high walls were covered with Indian wood, and the comfortable chairs were encrusted with silver and precious stones. Paintings and small pictures hung on the walls in a harmonious and orderly fashion. The outside entrance was made of polished marble shaded by the branches of old eucalyptus trees.

Abd al-Rahman pushed aside the muslin curtains and peered through the large balcony that overlooked the souk and saw women selling radishes, vegetables, and fresh figs from large baskets wrapped in checkered black scarves that they carried on their heads. Their children, with shaven heads, were breastfeeding. Customers, men and women, were moving among piles of lemons and oranges in huge wooden bowls, baskets of onions, green peppers, apples, and boxes of pressed dates. At the far end of the souk there were cages of ducks, hens, and small birds piled atop one another. Sheep were jumping at the railing of a bushy garden, a mysterious looking thicket where pots of basil and flowers were covered in shade.

Abd al-Rahman got dressed in front of the long armoire mirror in his warm bedroom. He tied his slim blue tie and slipped on his square eyeglasses with black plastic frames. He compared his reflection to Sartre's photograph hanging on the wall and was overwhelmed with sadness. What if I were one-eyed? The two of us would have looked alike! Abd al-Rahman had shaved his mustache and styled his hair like Sartre's. His handsome oval face reflected all of Sartre's features: a slim nose, slightly rounded cheeks, and a small mouth, all resulting in a similarity that fell short of being complete as long as he had both eyes. What would happen if he became one-eyed and turned into another Sartre? Abd al-Rahman felt at this moment the cruelty of existence; he thought that life was not fair. Had life been fair he, Abd al-Rahman, would have been born one-eyed, God would have made him so, like Jaseb, the vegetable seller of al-Sadriya souk. This illiterate, one-eyed man was not aware of his eye's Sartrian genius, the philosophical greatness of his imperfect eye, and the place of this imperfect eye in the history of philosophy. Jaseb preferred his good eye to his imperfect eye, unaware of the commonness and vulgarity of his good eye. He was usually sad, ashamed of his physical defect, living in a world where most people had two eyes, a world where everybody sought perfection.

Abd al-Rahman was well aware of the value and greatness of being one-eyed, but he knew that a metaphysical condition like that achieved by the god of knowledge, Sartre, was unattainable. He lost all hope of ever reaching that condition and felt his existence incomplete and dull. The sight of Jaseb tortured him, and he quarreled with him whenever he saw him. He swore at him, threatened him, and at the top of his lungs shouted at him, "By God, if it were not for that one eye of yours arguing in your favor, I would have smashed your head with my shoe."

Jaseb did not understand the philosopher's position toward his one eye and considered his words a bitter mockery of his physical defect. Abd al-Rahman would swear angrily at him, saying, "Damn your father and your father's father and Suhail Idris's father too!" Jaseb had no idea who Suhail Idris was, but realized that the man was responsible for the state of madness and loss that overcame people at that time. Jaseb listened carefully to the comments made by Shaul, the Jew who plotted against Arab existentialism. He was the source of the insults that Jaseb threw at his enemy, Abd al-Rahman, when he stood with his cart close to Shaul's shop in al-Sadriya souk.

Abd al-Rahman was haunted by his own binocular condition even while he was in Paris, the capital of existentialism, at the Sorbonne working toward his doctorate in existential philosophy in the late fifties. But he failed in his studies and returned home without a degree in French existentialism. Instead, like all Iraqis who seek knowledge overseas but return without a degree, he brought back a blonde French wife. Trying to console an Iraqi whose son returned home unsuccessful in his studies but lucky in love, Nouri al-Said commented to him, "Short of acquiring knowledge, at least marry someone from among the knowledge-able people."

No one at that time knew that Abd al-Rahman had very good and sound reasons for marrying a Frenchwoman. He would not have married Germaine had she been an ordinary woman with ordinary qualities. He did not marry her simply because she was blonde. He married her — and this very few people knew — because she was Sartre's compatriot.

Late one night Abd al-Rahman got lost in one of the dark alleys of Paris on his way home from a bout of drinking in a bar. He stood on a corner of the alley by a telephone pole in the pitch-black night as a cold wind whistled through the streets and a heavy fog settled softly over the city. He put his hands in his pockets, rolled up his coat collar, wrapped his scarf around his neck, and was trembling from cold, feeling the humidity seep through his shoes. He suddenly saw a young woman leaving a high-rise building. He stopped her to ask for directions home. She walked with him to his apartment.

Germaine was a modest young lady working as a babysit-ter for a weekly wage. She wasn't beautiful, but she was fair-skinned, blonde, and green-eyed. Abd al-Rahman was relieved when they reached the street that led to his apartment, and he asked her about her origins; it's a common practice among Iraqis upon meeting a foreigner to inquire about his tribe.

She was from Paris, she said, then turned to leave. Her words were like a revelation to him, a gift falling from the sky. He caught up with her and wouldn't let her go. "You must be an associate of Sartre's, aren't you?" he asked her, "Are you related to him?" The thin blonde girl was surprised. She had never heard the name Sartre. She shook her shoulders in astonishment as she looked at the face of the man sinking into his black coat between the white collar and the scarf.

"Oh! You do not know Sartre! Sheikh Hani Halil wrote a response to his work in three volumes, entitled, *The obliterating and crushing response to the straying Jean son of Paul son of Sartre*."

She inquired, extremely amused, "Who is this Sheikh?"

Surprised, Abd al-Rahman wondered aloud, "Oh! You do not know Sheikh Hani Halil either! He's a famous scholar. He was a student at Najaf, who nearly caused a diplomatic incident between France and Iraq with his book."

The truth of the matter was that Abd al-Rahman was enamored of the great French philosopher and his philosophy but never managed to meet him during his stay in Paris. He had seen Sartre a few times on the Boulevard Saint-Michel, in the Latin Quarter, at the Sorbonne, at the Café Nîme in Montparnasse, in Saint-Germain-des-Prés, and browsing through books displayed on the quay of the Seine. Abd al-Rahman was intimidated by Sartre, feared him, and every time he got close to the philosopher, he trembled with fear and left without speaking to him.

There were reasons for this fear. One was that Abd al-Rahman's French was not strong enough to allow him to engage in any kind of debate with the philosopher. During his stay in Paris he failed to master the language, despite serious efforts to learn it. He could only discuss general topics and had difficulty reading literary and philosophical texts. His professor at the university strongly advised him to master French, explaining that he would not be able to study French philosophy with a weak and shaky comprehension of the language.

He saw in the skinny girl a conversation partner, one with whom he could discuss philosophy as much as he liked, the same way he boasted to the prostitutes who visited his apartment. They were not at all concerned with the veracity or quality of his arguments. He was mistaken in thinking that Germaine believed him when, at the end of their steamy sexual encounters during which he demonstrated his virility, he would tell her that he was nauseated.

Everything around him made him feel the meaninglessness of existence and thus nauseated him. Feverish lovemaking with the girl made him sick. The piece of red steak he gluttonously ate and washed down with red wine made him sick. As did the high-quality cigarettes he avidly smoked. His wanderings in the Bois de Boulogne, the easy pleasures of the Latin Quarter, the x-rated movies in Saint-Michel, shiny shoes, silk neckties, and strong perfumes—everything made him sick.

Despite her very modest education, the girl he befriended was not fooled by his declarations. She had vast experience in life. She could not believe that a person who devoured life as he did would experience what the foolish philosophers were calling nausea. But she pretended to believe him and his philosophy, his madness and his stupidities. Sometimes at the end of their lovemaking, as she slipped out of bed and put on her bright red slip, she would admit to feeling funny. She described it as a strange feeling, something she never experienced before, something like nausea.

Abd al-Rahman returned to Baghdad for good in the early sixties, accompanied by his French wife and justifying his life as a philosopher without a degree. He was warmly welcomed and supported by his country's intellectuals, to whom he declared that it did not make sense to have a degree in a senseless world, a phrase that became famous. Someone in his entourage would speculate, "With or without a degree, was Sartre a philosopher?" This scene had taken place on a very hot summer evening his first year home from Paris. He was at the Café Brazil with Salman al-Safi and Abbas Philosophy. The two men got very excited, overturned their chairs, and shouted their approval of this extraordinary philosophical phrase. The philosopher moved them deeply with his appearance and intoxicated them with his philosophical features.

Abbas Philosophy and Salman became the most important intellectuals of the sixties. Abbas came to Baghdad from
Kirkuk, after a career in the petroleum industry, to start his
career as a poet. Because rhymed poetry posed a problem for
him, he championed free verse and followed in the footsteps
of an entire generation. At that time he used to call Sartre
"Kaka Sartre." Salman came from al-Shatra, with a small sum
of money, to study at Baghdad University. He was like many
country people who move to the city, dark-skinned and timid,
motivated by dreams of relationships with the most beautiful
girls in town, chosen from the bourgeoisie to overcome a psychological gap. If they failed to establish such a relation due to
their inexperience, gaucherie, and lack of qualifications, they
would invent one in their imaginations and nourish their dreams
with love disputes, neurotic fights, tears, and submission. Once
those delusions thinned, they'd encounter reality and run away,
accusing the girl—to whom they had never spoken—of betrayal
and deception and accuse her family of committing social dis-
crimination, and of having a disgusting bourgeois mentality and
sickening aristocratic airs.

Salman left the university and found a job as an assistant
tailor in Hassoun al-Hindi's boutique on al-Rashid Street, near
al-Zawraa cinema. He planned to devote time to writing a major
novel condemning the feudal system in the Muntafik brigade.

The young Iraqi intellectuals celebrated the great philosophy of existentialism, the subject of articles by Suhail Idris in
al-Adab journal since the fifties and by Abd al-Rahman Badawi
in *al-Katib al-'arabi* since the forties. Iraqi intellectuals became
acquainted with that philosophy after the Second World War
in the Waqwaq café, near the Olympic Club in Antar Square.
Abd al-Rahman returned from Paris in the sixties and told Iraqis
about his personal experiences and what he had learned of that
philosophy. He rented an elegant house for his French wife in

Mahallet al-Sadriya and became the uncontested existential philosopher. He was renowned in the Arab World and even received an invitation from Suhail Idris to write articles on existentialism for *al-Adab,* the most famous Arab existentialist journal of the time. I never found the letter sent by Idris and also signed by his wife Aida among the manuscripts I have, though when I met them at the restaurant in al-Camp both Salman and Abbas assured me that they had read the letter. Abd al-Rahman arrogantly declined Suhail Idris's invitation on the grounds that his philosophical thinking occurred in French and he was unable to translate it into Arabic.

The truth is that Abd al-Rahman was unable to write in French or Arabic. His thinking was disorganized, and he was unable to express his feelings in either language. His education was superficial and not derived from books. It was the same education that characterized most of the intellectuals of his generation; it consisted of hours in the morning spent talking, playing dominos, and smoking a water pipe at the café, going to the movies in the afternoon to stretch lazily on the comfortable chairs, and spending evenings drinking and gambling in bars. They only knew the titles of books and what had been written in newspaper reviews. With words they built up kingdoms and knocked down others, ruined reputations, while in their own lives they were unable to carry out what they planned, change their realities, or even comprehend their own environment.

Abd al-Rahman's argument against writing was, in fact, quite valid, an existentially reasonable argument. He claimed that whoever writes finds something worthwhile, a meaningful life, and expects some financial reward. "How could I then go on believing in a meaningless world?" he would ask. People hailed this concept, and a whole generation of intellectuals did not write because they didn't want to be part of this false, deceptive world, they didn't want to be cheated, they didn't want to be part of the complex imposed by colonialism, reactionaries, and the ungrateful.

The truth was totally different. Abd al-Rahman was unable to spend hours sitting at a desk to write or even to lie on his stomach on the floor. On the other hand, he liked reading because reading was like dreaming. He used to go over the first few lines of a text and forget the world around him, totally lost in his thoughts. He would start pacing back and forth in his room, get dressed, and roam aimlessly in the streets of the city, dreaming of the words he had read or of the words he intended to say.

Abd al-Rahman found talking to be both soothing and entertaining. Conversation kept him company and pleased him because words, as most of his companions discovered, are like thoughts in their potential to signify meaning. They conform to every aspect of awareness. This is so because the speaker begins the process of thinking the instant he utters a word. At that moment he's enthusiastic and powerful—or perhaps he is a doubter or denier. Writing is different, a distinct form, far removed from spoken words. It distances itself from emotional reactions. It's like masturbation. It represents a feel for the image but not the image itself, while spoken words are, at the very least, an agreement between the image and the object, between the moment and the reaction, the thought and the soul. When Abd al-Rahman speaks, he allows his words to float freely while he feels a kind of purification or numbness. The words he utters and the feelings he experiences evaporate. Thoughts that struggle in his mind fly away. This is how Abd al-Rahman used to talk, because spoken words offered him a true nihilism, not an approximation, a realistic philosophy rather than figurative thinking. In short, Abd al-Rahman was a speaker not a writer; he was a philosopher not a scoundrel.

Ismail Hadoub asked him one day, "What about Sartre? Why does he write?" and closed his eyes to await the philosopher's response. Abd al-Rahman replied, also with closed eyes, and like a prophet, and said, "Sartre is one thing and we are something else. What is given to Sartre is not given to anyone else. Sartre writes to have his books translated into Arabic so that we may read them. Otherwise, pray tell, if Sartre did not write, how could we have heard of him? Sartre is something else," he said as he was walking with Ismail Hadoub on a very cold winter night, down al-Rashid Street near the Haydar Khana mosque. They were soon joined by the turbaned men who emerged from the large wooden gates of the mosque. They crowded the narrow sidewalk near the metal ramp, decorated with Islamic designs and blue enamel. Abd al-Rahman crossed to the other side of the street once he spotted this swarm of white turbans, gray waistcoats, and black gowns. They all looked alike: each with a Quran and prayer beads in hand, with beards and quick, self-confident steps and stern looks. No sooner did they step down from the sidewalk, however, than a small black carriage pulled by two white horses stopped in front of them; a lady wearing the traditional burqa and black abaya stepped out. Abd al-Rahman and Ismail hired the carriage for a ride across the city before going to Dalal Masabni's Grief Adab nightclub near the Roxy cinema.

They were both silent as they soaked in pleasure, taking in the streets lined with high-rise buildings and admiring the sidewalks canopied with eucalyptus trees. Behind the two men, the minarets and silent green domes of the mosques reached into the air. The streets were lit with kerosene lamps that guided pedestrians on foggy nights. They took in the scene unfolding on the sidewalks crowded with water pipes and waiters serving cups of tea to elegant customers in western dress. They had to walk close to the moss that grew in the mud breaking through the cracks of the asphalt sidewalks. Unveiled women crowded the cafés and groceries in the markets. Some sat on their doorsteps. It was a common scene at that time: the Royal and Roxy cinemas, the Mackenzie and Coronet bookstores, the Swiss café, Orosdi Back department store, Sartre, and Trotsky. Throughout that decade Abd al-Rahman was like a crocodile with tears constantly in his eyes. As he walked, his eyes would wander left and right, fixing on women with big breasts revealed by low-cut dresses. He stared at their soft bodies and golden legs, the denim skirts, the shiny umbrellas.

2

The philosopher of al-Sadriya was not short on despondent friends, but he needed a public post and had to write articles to introduce himself to society. He was handsome and appealed to women, and men were impressed by his elegance. He had money to spend on prostitutes. He was smart, funny, and, indeed, quite popular among the literary café-goers. At that time, it pleased society men to encounter a young Baghdadi who was capable of engaging the greatest western philosophers and thinkers, including Sartre. They took special pleasure in seeing him sitting alone in a corner, meditating on existence and its nihilistic nature. They enjoyed listening to his strange language, difficult and complicated, about existence by and for itself. For his part, he enjoyed his quick fame and prominence. He was proud of his social class, but he was a modest philosopher who had acquired some French manners: simple elegance, well chosen words, and mannerisms that were usually lost when he drank. He was hoping for a prominent position, real power, and resounding fame, but his awareness of his shortcomings had convinced him that a philosopher does not work, he philosophizes.

In 1957, on a visit to Baghdad while still a student in Paris, his father introduced him to Prime Minister Nouri al-Said, hoping to secure a position for him upon his return to the country, to serve as a philosopher in the cabinet of ministers.

The brilliant politician took great interest in him and gave him a piece of advice he never forgot, "You are a philosopher, and you must continue to do your philosophy. Work would interfere with your activities as a philosopher. An office job is not for you, and you can do without it. Work is for creatures like us who are not capable of such noble and great thinking."

Abd al-Rahman was relieved to hear these words. His father had placed him in a rather delicate situation, from which the prime minister had in fact freed him. His father, however, did not share his relief but, rather, was depressed, angry, and resentful; he was convinced that the prime minister felt threatened by his son's genius. The prime minister, on the other hand, remarked in his memoirs of the year 1957 (a modest notebook that was in the possession of Mrs. Amna al-Said), that, "The honorable Shawkat Amin often burdens me with suggestions that, if I were to apply them, would turn the political situation upside down and destroy us. Today he brought me his son, the one we got rid of by sending him off to study philosophy in Paris. He suggested that we appoint him as the cabinet's philosopher after his return from Paris. I explained to him delicately that appointing a philosopher to the cabinet would not bolster its survival. What's more alarming is the fact that his son returned from Paris worse off than he was before he went. As soon as I heard the young man speak I became convinced that, without a doubt, he was crazy. If he is not crazy then I am crazy. By God, I wonder how these riffraff became aristocrats!"

The prime minister's remark was certainly biased, out of place, and unfair, as he did not know that Abd al-Rahman, notable philosopher that he was, actually shied away from relations with influential people and prominent families. He even despised their way of life. He sought to promote a society that protected his imagination from pedestrian thinking. The aristocracy did not fit this requirement by any measure. Had he told the prime minister that he felt nauseated, surely he would have been met with ridicule and bitter sarcasm. Although he desired aristocratic women, he also loved to humiliate them. Had he married one, she would have been honored, but he chose to marry a western woman who surpassed them in manners and philosophy. He wanted to humiliate and ignore them and showcase his superior philosophical thinking. The women who surrounded his mother considered this cheating.

Despite feeling nausea, a nihilistic sentiment regarding existence and the futility of life, Abd al-Rahman was not devoid of love for the high life: dancing in nightclubs, drinking cognac, and joking with the waiters, the dancers, and the drunks. Dalal Masabni took pride in being among his intellectual group and complained to everyone about his nausea and her own. But she also enjoyed life, sought pleasure, and wore heavy makeup. She brimmed with desire and excitement, strove to make a living, and enjoyed alcohol, drugs, and music. Abd al-Rahman gravitated toward that life along with Ismail, whom he used to push into a taxi in front of King Ghazi Park saying, "Let's spend two to three hours nauseated."

Grief Adab was decorated with photographs of half-naked dancers and licentious ads that promised a memorable time with the dancers, whether it be "Tear of the Eyes," "Sugar of the Heart," or "Virgin of Existentialism!" This last name was suggested, naturally, by Abd al-Rahman. He even suggested that the hallway that led to the dance hall be decorated with a large portrait of Jean-Paul Sartre opposite a red lantern. Dalal Masabni agreed without discussion. Abd al-Rahman brought a large photograph of the French philosopher in a thin golden frame. The dancers, led by Dalal, received him with cheers. Abd al-Rahman climbed up on a small stool to hang the photograph, while Ismail helped him straighten it. When Dalal asked about the identity of the man in the photograph, Abd al-Rahman smiled sadly and bent his head. As he moved his finger to point, it fell exactly on Sartre's cross-eye. He told her, "My dear Dalal, this is the man who taught us all to feel nauseated." She shook her head, "Oh, then this is the original nauseated person."

Such was the extent of Dalal's understanding of the matter, and among all the dancers whose mouths dropped as they considered that mysterious, beautiful photograph, only Ismail was aware of the importance of the moment. Dancing and cheering, they celebrated Sartre's arrival, then walked through the long hallway between rows of photographs of half-naked dancers, surrounded by frenzied customers, with drinks in hand.

Abd al-Rahman and Ismail's regular table was at the far end of the room. The table had a sacred history dating back to the first day Abd al-Rahman entered the club, and it became known as the philosopher's table. That day a fat, big-breasted, and fair-skinned redhead was singing in a plaintive voice as the crowd enthusiastically cheered her on. As the customers exchanged their greetings, she seized the opportunity to welcome the arrival of the al-Sadriya philosopher, Abd al-Rahman Sartre, which she pronounced "Santer." With his very first drink Abd al-Rahman turned into a powerful and authentic philosopher; Ismail, on the other hand, had a higher tolerance, as he had started drinking in his youth. Ismail was infatuated with a young Assyrian dancer nicknamed Wazzeh (Duck). She looked like a white duck, and everything on her body moved when she walked: her breasts, hips, and restless feet. She constantly chewed gum. She had memorized a dictionary of depraved words, and every now and then she would point to her half-naked breasts—which Ismail described as "an existentialist bosom"—and tell everyone that it was there that nausea reposed. This always provoked a huge uproar in the hall.

Abd al-Rahman was in the habit of ordering drinks and food from Mikha the server. His table was usually filled with glasses of cognac and whiskey, pistachios, salad, fava beans, and chicken. Ismail was usually busy smelling the dancer's dyed and unkempt hair and trying to kiss the Virgin of Existentialism's neck. Abd al-Rahman demeaned himself before her; he would kneel in front of the dancer and flirt in a manner that naturally upset Ismail. Every now and then she would whisper something in his ear, her breath smelling of cheap cognac. He would laugh loudly and beat the table so hard that the cigarette butts in the ashtray would fly all over the table. Whenever the philosopher touched Wazzeh's naked shoulders, she would laugh her frivolous laugh, adding to the impact of the loud music that fired up the place and tickled the philosopher's senses. He would sing a song in French and tell his friends that it was the existentialist anthem, puzzling them with his incomprehensible French philosophy sung to a manic tune. Alcohol increased their nausea, and their eyes twinkled upon hearing this great philosophy.

During one of those evenings at the nightclub, Ismail shouted, "Women—nothing matters in life but women and alcohol . . . ." No sooner had Abd al-Rahman heard these words, in fact before his companion could even finish his sentence, the philosopher stood up in anger. He wiped his forehead with his hairy, shaking hand, causing the place to come to a standstill. Everybody was terrified. He asked Ismail, "Have you forgotten existentialism, you son of a bitch? Has a dancer blotted out everything I've taught you?" Ismail was dumbfounded by Abd al-Rahman's accusatory, high-strung tone. He lowered his head, and his shiny black hair fell over his eyes. He lit a cigarette with an unsteady hand, looked at Abd al-Rahman with drunken eyes, and said, "Oh no, Abd al-Rahman, philosopher of al-Sadriya, Sartre of the Arabs. I am nauseated, and this woman is existentialism personified. As for me, I am existence for existence's sake."

These existential words, these philosophical sentences and deep Sartrian thoughts calmed Abd al-Rahman, while the poor dancers, the truly existential creatures, looked on, puzzled by this world turned upside down. They felt reassured, however, that the matter was solved with those magical words, and so they returned to their carousal. Abd al-Rahman, in contrast, was transported by Ismail's response into his memories of the Jussieux nightclub in the Latin Quarter. He remembered the international fair in Montmartre, dancing gypsies moving as gracefully as tobacco leaves. The gypsy songs excited him and revived the memory of the enigmatic Parisian scenery composed of existentialism, garrulity, Latin philosophies, and women's clothes decorated with layers of red lace. He said to Ismail, "Let's transform Baghdad into another Paris. Let's make it a second Paris, the capital of existentialism." Surprised, Ismail wondered how this could be done.

It was the sight of the Negro dancer from Basra that inspired in Abd al-Rahman the idea of a national existentialist movement. Her feminine, uninhibited dancing, the way she jumped up on the stage and revealed her brown body shining under the light, her thick lips and ivory white teeth, and her fishy smell—all this inflamed Abd al-Rahman's imagination. He asked Ismail, "Who says that existentialism is not concerned with politics and national unity? Otherwise, what would Sartrian commitment mean?"

After a paralyzing silence, an angel's silence, Abd al-Rahman ordered the waiter to call the dancers, Dam' al-Ain, Wazzeh, Rizan the Kurd and her Arabic music ensemble, Lamia, Munibeh, and Saniya. He then declared the establishment of a National Existentialism for the unity of the people, with Sartre's blessing. The nightclub turned into a wrestling arena, chairs and tables were up-ended, liquor bottles smashed, and plates of appetizers flew across the hall and skidded along the floor. Customers escaped through a side door, and the prostitutes were shouting. The waiters and cashiers were yelling at the top of their lungs. The dancers swayed like madwomen to the beat of the wild music and eventually fell to the floor. Abd al-Rahman and Ismail collapsed from excessive drinking and fatigue; the waiters picked them up and dumped them outside.

3

A few hours later a taxi drove Abd al-Rahman home. He was drunk, with a cigarette still in his mouth, and his jacket hung on his finger. Ismail had to push him out of the car. No sooner had he knocked on the door than he collapsed on the stoop. Moments later, while he was still on the ground, the iron door opened slowly. He had difficulty seeing through his liquor-induced haze but was able to make out Germaine standing over him in her nightgown.

The philosopher was an extreme existentialist. He was not looking for suffering in love or even the torture of impossible love. He considered love, like everything else, nonexistent, simply an unformed, unmaterialized feeling, because love is simply a part of nihilism, and nihilism alone was the essence of everything. To him, Germaine's presence was delusive, as was her absence. Like everything that surrounded him, she was an illusion. The philosopher made fun of organic fusion in love, metempsychosis, and closeness in love because none of these things existed. For him to philosophize about love he had first to reinvent love, to purify it of the sterility that the idealists had forced onto it. He had to cleanse love of the misunderstandings, the isolation, and the disappointments it faced. According to him every failed love was a sick love—it carried nothing but ugliness. He knew that Germaine was ugly, but her ugliness was a form of beauty particular to her. After having slept with her countless times, he forgot her ugliness and even got used to it. What did belief in love bring him other than regret? Love is a lie, and only the nihilism it provokes can be considered real.

The philosopher did not lack the tactical skills to establish a sharp correlation between truth and deceit. The amazing secret to his behavior was his ability to hide his feelings and to deceive. His primary deceitful attitude was vis-à-vis his wife, whom he did not love and this is where his philosophical game in life begins. Whenever his role as a lover was pure and acceptable, he discarded the minor mistakes he made and the flowery words he uttered. He hid behind and from them, and moved constantly within this closed cycle where he found himself and to which he had become used. Yet he had to find a strategy to deal with Germaine.

He had to adopt a special system with Germaine. He would show eagerness and compliance whenever she rejected him and disregard her whenever she submitted to him; he would erase her from his imagination and fling her far away. He liked this game and spent time thinking and plotting. He took special pleasure in his thoughts as he formulated and refined them. He looked forward to the morning, when he would apply the ideas conceived the night before. The fact of the matter, though, was that it was not he who planned and plotted, but rather that he executed what Germaine had planned for him. She was very smart and made him believe that he was the master of the situation, that it was he who planned and plotted and had the last word. But it was an illusion. He was manipulated; he was an object not a subject. He had no idea that the decisions he executed were hers, not his.

Germaine was a dangerous strategist, capable of devising extraordinary plans of great consequence. She knew what she wanted just as much as the philosopher did not know what he wanted. The road to their aspirations led through opposite gates, one distant, the other difficult, complex, and requiring a great deal of effort to reach. In her genius Germaine was able to bring the two gates close enough to be fused into one. She had no intention of revealing her thinking to him, and she never talked with him about what might be her final goal, or ideal, akin to the philosopher's idealism that he denied. Germaine was not an idealist like him, and the only abstract terms in her vocabulary pertained to geographical locations, such as the northern hemisphere and the equator. Her drive to reach her goal was not insignificant, nor was she stupid or disinterested. She was well aware that the road led either east or west, with no exit in between. She and her husband were different, with different characters. She was exceptionally self-controlled, and her uniqueness was more clearly defined than his. Although they didn't admit it to one another, they were both aware of their shared tendency to pretend to possess things they did not have. It was instinctive. Each was aware that the other was not gifted, but Germaine was different from the philosopher because she could distinguish between the logical and the ordinary. This was the so-called experimental French thinking that Germaine understood instinctually. Pretending to ignore the discrepancies would only prolong this situation. Germaine did not confuse matters. She placed everything in its appropriate place. She had weighed matters very carefully and assessed them in a cautious, Cartesian manner. The choice was between, on the one hand, housekeeping in Paris, cleaning the apartments of wage-earners, and submitting to the whims of those whose pockets were bursting with their wealth. The other path led to marriage with the sensitive Middle Eastern fellow enamored of existentialism, an elegant and fashionable man, who belonged to an aristocratic family, and was connected with the Baghdad elite. On top of all that he had a special place in the Eastern City.

This Cartesian Frenchwoman was faced with a choice between two totally different lives but could select only one. The first option was biological: love or the mere perpetuation of the human race. The second was social and would bring wealth. She chose the latter. She realized the wisdom of her choice when

Abd al-Rahman visited her apartment and brought her a huge bouquet. He then asked her timidly, "Do you like escarole?" to which she replied with her head bent in affected embarrassment, "Yes." At this moment Abd al-Rahman took a bag from the pocket of his black coat, placed it on the table, and poured two glasses of champagne. He adjusted the white rose in his buttonhole, moved to the far end of the room, and took out candles and dishes from the drawer where Germaine kept them neatly wrapped in a piece of cloth. He placed them in front of her and asked, "Germaine, will you marry me?" to which she replied, "I'll think about it."

Germaine didn't have a negative view of Baghdad. She didn't find it particularly ugly nor did she suffer from its burning heat or its people who were so different from the French. Abd al-Rahman provided her with a large, luxurious house in Mahallet al-Sadriya, surrounded by trees and a brick wall. His father was the first to bless the house where he expected his grandchildren to be born, those who would perpetuate his name and memory. Abd al-Rahman's father was convinced of his son's genius and respected him for his mind, but also because he had married a Frenchwoman. He considered his son's marriage to a Frenchwoman a distinction that could not be matched. For him it signified that fashionable, brilliant Europe appreciated and respected his son by marrying off one of its daughters to him. He saw it as a family alliance between him and de Gaulle, rather than the mere fact that a young man had met a woman in Paris while studying there and brought her home. His father therefore busied himself furnishing the house to suit the tastes of his son's French wife. He was determined to provide her with everything and did not want to appear stingy. She, on the other hand, was annoyed by his excessive generosity and his continuous intrusions into their lives, yet she accepted his help and showed appreciation and respect for his feelings.

Germaine liked this strange, oriental-looking Mahalleh district with its narrow winding streets. In the souk she felt like a tourist in the city she had read about, the Baghdad of the *One Thousand and One Nights*. She imagined herself a Christian prisoner locked in her quarters by an oriental prince. She had to compartmentalize her thinking: one mode of thinking was incredibly sarcastic; the other allowed her to pretend to experience nausea, in order to please her husband. She was able to hide her sarcasm during the first year of their marriage, and so the time passed without major incident. She pleased her husband's existential tastes in various ways. This lasted until she gave birth in Paris to twins, a girl and a boy. When she called her husband and anxiously asked him what he wanted to call the children, he told her, "call the boy Abath (Absurdity) and the girl Suda (Nothingness)." When he translated the meaning of the names, she slammed the receiver and broke down crying. She felt the loneliness she had known before and realized that the mind she had split in two had rejoined itself.

She was vexed and disgusted, even angry, but she controlled herself because she was well aware that her husband was serious and inflexible. She realized that an existentialist is truly obsessed, and even sick, with no hope of a cure. Her punishment for him was to put an end to her affected nausea when she returned to Baghdad. She neither cared for his philosophy nor for him. She lived her life with total disregard for existentialism. She was totally cured and concentrated her efforts on raising her children to prevent them from becoming like their father, making sure that they did not become fanatical believers in anything. In order to take proper care of her children she needed to take care of herself and her health. She took extreme care of her skin, her hair, and her figure, remaining slim and agile, exercising every day, eating at regular hours, and taking hot baths. She was obsessed with the European fear of aging, of death, and anything reminding her of death, sickness, or the gradual disintegration of the body.

There was no room for the philosopher in his own house. There was no nausea or any other external manifestation of existentialism. Germaine left everything behind in Paris. For Abd al-Rahman, love with a woman devoid of philosophy was meaningless. So he was compelled to search for his nausea elsewhere, which naturally led him to Sherif and Haddad's bar on al-Rashid Street and the Café Brazil. But at night, his nausea only manifested itself at the Grief Adab nightclub and with its owner, the dancer Dalal Masabni.

4

Dalal was a Christian dancer who had received her training in Beirut from one of al-Hamra Street's most famous dancers. Although she experienced nausea, especially when she was in the company of the philosopher, she also suffered from a malaise, a sickness of the century. The philosopher told her that she had a Chateaubriand air, but the truth is that she was young and seductive. Frankly, although Dalal was intensely attracted to Hadoub's virility, she was just as attracted to the philosopher's open pocket.

Dalal felt compelled to accommodate her customers by sharing their feelings, so each time she slept with the philosopher she confessed to a strong feeling of nausea. This attracted the philosopher to her, especially because his wife's feeling of nausea had disappeared since she had returned from Paris. He explained his wife's condition by saying that Baghdad lacked the existential atmosphere that in Paris fostered such pure philosophical sensations.

When Abd al-Rahman asked his wife to explain why she experienced such an intense nausea in Paris but none at all in

Baghdad, she smiled and said, "Simply put, I had not lost my strong existential feeling then." This compelled the philosopher to look for someone else because he couldn't bear the idea of an individually experienced nausea. He used to compare the nausea to a kiss that has to be shared by a man and a woman. Germaine and he had stopped having sex, especially after the birth of the twins, Abath and Suda. When one day he insisted on his rights she shouted in his face, "I am raising your Abath and Suda, so deal with your nausea alone. This is a fair division of labor. You did not worry about Abath, who caught German measles, or Suda, who didn't stop crying for two days. I spent a whole day in Dr. Simon Bahlawan's clinic. So take your nausea elsewhere and leave me in peace."

He did not appreciate her critical arguments at all, which shed doubt on all aspects of existentialism, against his philosophy. He swallowed her attacks calmly and put down *Les chemins de la liberté*. He rearranged the black-framed eyeglasses that resembled Sartre's, got dressed, and left in a hurry. He walked down King Ghazi Street just as the street sweeper was pushing the garbage in front of him. He quickened his step to avoid the debris but didn't make it. Instead, he ended up inhaling the dust and fell victim to an allergy attack. He headed toward the entertainment district, where movie houses advertised films with posters and neon lights. The sight of a yellowing leaf on a branch, a feather on a shop awning, or a fruit peel crushed by pedestrians, left him nauseated. He longed for the change of seasons and for a nausea that combined all his pleasures into a single experience, derived from all his senses. He hoped for an emotion that would enliven and tickle his mind.

Abd al-Rahman found great pleasure in his own nausea, but not Sartre's, as an expression of his complex and muddled feelings. This nausea allowed him his first opportunity to convey what was going on in his little head. Through it he was able to choose, think, and be content, after having spent his childhood and adolescence oppressed, repressed, and unable to express his thoughts freely. Nausea was a new channel through which he could associate sight and smell, two senses that mingled to form one indescribable impression. It flavored an idea, and allowed it to be presented in a uniquely charming way, deep and mysterious. This is the feeling that Abd al-Rahman adopted in his philosophy and named nausea.

This feeling of nausea was a great mystery to his contemporaries. It mellowed every one of his emotional reactions, which were otherwise characterized by roughness and gibberish. Philosophy was Abd al-Rahmans's aim, the philosophy he sought and enthralled him. He considered the waiting time for the realization of this objective a philosophical waiting rather than a spontaneous moment. His description of that moment was of a philosophical nature rather than a metaphysical philosophy, one that brought elevated concepts down to earth. It was a philosophy that intermingled with existing earthly matters.

Abd al-Rahman saw the change of seasons as nihilistic, as he observed trees losing their leaves, soft and shiny flowers falling to the ground at the slightest touch, petals spreading over the pond, and the reflection of their color in the glass window. Each of those natural occurences had a nihilistic dimension that, since he married Germaine and moved with her into this big house overlooking the souk, manifested itself every day in spring. It appeared in the space between the branches and the sky, between the high and the low, and after a light rain.

He considered the catkin the most beautiful flower on earth because of all flowers—roses, white and lavender lilacs, and jasmines—it was only the catkin that helped him experience an even deeper nausea. He had a special affection for catkins and defined them in philosophical terms, "the catkins were existential flowers before existential philosophy itself came to be." The flower allowed him to perceive the nihilism of existence that emerged along with the appearance of humanity. He used to ask the gardener for a sprig that he would keep in his room to ensure that he would always feel nauseated, even in his dreams. He dreamed his garden was filled with them or that they wrapped around the fence. He would stare at them in his sleep and feel such a strong, painful desire he was moved to shout out loud.

The philosopher liked many things, especially those that enhanced his nausea, such as fresh cream covered with cherry jam. He liked it and ate it almost every day. The combination of the two colors, white and dark red, reminded him of the color of the wine that Jean-Paul Sartre used to drink on Saint-Germain-des-Prés. This delicious similarity contributed to his understanding of Sartre's mood. It gave him a memory of gluttonous existentialism, suitable for a man who loved food, drink, and good health.

Abd al-Rahman's existentialism was earthy, organized, and spontaneous. It led to the perfection of the self, not its degradation, to the elevation of the soul, not its destruction. Existentialism provided him with the best in life, a wonderful time, unique moments, and total and complete pleasures. His might be described as a lustful existentialism, whose nausea engendered life, not death and suicide. It led to heavy and delicious meals, crazy nights of drinking, and pulling his mistress's hair while removing her lace panties. It inspired him to cheer and shout like common people.

Abd al-Rahman's existentialism was limitless; it transcended all boundaries. His nausea contained an unbelievable sweetness, irresistible desire, and ineffable rejoicing. He acted a bit strange in his nauseated condition: he would slump onto a carriage driver, fall heavily on the seat, roll over into the stagnant water of the sidewalk, or fall from his bed or in the garden. He did not need to be artificially elevated to experience this happiness, which is purer than any joy. He needed a great spontaneity to know this happiness. He believed that there were two types of threats to the mind: external events that might hamper the progress of nausea and internal matters that caused him to forget, even for a second, the nausea.

During a bout of heavy drinking he might forget to express himself and tell those around him that he suffers from what philosophy refers to as nausea. Once he recovered from his drunkenness, most often in his room, and remembered, it would be too late. His mood would darken, and he would become angry with himself because he had failed to detect his nauseated state as it happened and thus had lost it. There were occasions when Abd al-Rahman forgot to express this feeling clearly, and he felt it slip away. In fact, it was the philosopher himself who sometimes neglected this feeling once he became absorbed in and crushed by worldly matters. He allowed himself only a minimum amount of worry about experiencing an anxious, dazed happiness caused by some accidental event. The happiness he experienced was most likely the result of pure nervousness, a condition that made it impossible for him to capture the feeling during moments of intense and total enjoyment. Thus the eternal feeling of nausea became a temporary one, while the philosopher preferred a timeless nausea, as did existential thought. This fleeting, beautiful, nauseating moment melted too fast, like butter in seawater, whereas the philosopher would have liked it to be everlasting, eternal. He often said to Ismail Hadoub, "What if man stayed in a state of nausea from birth to death?" Hadoub was surprised and asked, "How could that be?" and wrote down the philosopher's reply.

In response to Hadoud's astonishment, Abd al-Rahman offered a lengthy explanation, "For example, drinking brandy like this excellent vintage, or smoking Dutch tobacco like the fine stuff I have now in my pipe, or resting on the chest of a woman like Dalal (whose breasts protrude like two blown balloons), then experiencing a high and permanent degree of nausea. Drinking, smoking, and resting on a woman's chest until death would be permanent nausea, a moment fixed in time while the world goes forward. This would mean the actualization of a complete existentialism, and thus one would become the greatest existentialist on earth."

As he concluded, he shook his head, threw it back in a philosophical manner, and lapsed into a state of anxious silence. His words touched Ismail Hadoub deeply. "This is what escaped Sartre. He didn't pay attention to it, isn't that so?"

"No, he did not," Abd al-Rahman replied, "but I would like to transmit my thoughts to those who worship existentialism. I would like to introduce them to my existential thinking because existentialism is an open pleasure, a general one, not individual or selfish. In other words it is a selfish pleasure made for others to enjoy. We will establish an Arab existentialism with its own character. We want to promulgate it and distinguish it from western existentialism as Sartre defined it."

Ismail Hadoub rushed to write down these complex comments, words that were incomprehensible to him, puzzling philosophical declarations. They didn't require proof; they were self-explanatory through their complexity alone. Ismail understood philosophy as something that was impossible to understand, which explained the attractive and fascinating nature of Abd al-Rahman's words. He used to utter incomprehensible and unknown words that gave him certain superiority over his peers. He was lost in a philosophical fog, and through it was able to achieve success. The situation reassured the philosopher's parents, but he was concerned with his own personal fate. He knew that his ability to express mysterious ideas gave him the power to control weak characters even if stronger minds denounced him. He masked his position with the excuse that our society was not philosophical.

Ismail Hadoub wrote down everything the philosopher said. He didn't want to lose a single word. He was the only one convinced that Abd al-Rahman was a giant thinker who deserved to be believed and followed. He was a philosopher, and Ismail was devoid of philosophy; he was wealthy and could spend money, whereas Ismail was poor and couldn't find anything to eat. Abd al-Rahman resembled Sartre, but Ismail did not; he looked like himself. Abd al-Rahman was married to Sartre's cousin, but Ismail was a single man hunting for a rich wife.

The differences between the two men were tangible, and both were well aware of them. Philosophy could not erase those social disparities but in fact deepened and strengthened them. Each was aware of his true circumstance, his social status, and each tried to delineate his life according to this contradiction. Abd al-Rahman liked to distance himself from his class. He avoided and disliked his social class and never failed to express his feelings toward it. His attitude constantly called to mind his membership in the elite class, and it reminded those around him of the refinement of his class and its arrogance. For these reasons he sought to climb down the social ladder and become part of the lower classes. Only those who are highly placed want to go down—a natural inclination. Ismail, on the other hand, wanted to climb up the ladder because he was affiliated with the lower stratum of society. Thus the difference between those who climb up the ladder and those who come down is social and not philosophical. It's an economic difference, if we consider the significance of the matter. It's the difference between rich and poor, or beggar and donor, regardless of the nature of the donation, whether it's material or philosophical. This made Abd al-Rahman the donor and Ismail the beggar, since Abd al-Rahman was the philosopher and Ismail a mere follower.

5

Ismail Hadoub was not pampered or philosophical like Abd al-
Rahman, the philosopher. He appeared on the Baghdad scene in
the mid-fifties as a salesman selling pornographic photographs.
In his early days in Baghdad he did not have anything regular to
eat or drink or even a place to sleep. He ate whatever he could
lay his hands on, and that meant leftovers and garbage from rich
people's kitchens. He drank the dregs of arrack left in bottles
thrown near bars, and he slept wherever he could. He took odd
jobs: selling pornography, carrying luggage at modest hotels,
cutting glass in al-Jam market, sweeping for the municipality,
and sometimes working as a servant in rich people's homes. He
had an inclination for pleasure, amusement, and a vagabond life.
He wandered the streets and picked pockets in bus stations. He
lived in cheap, dirty, half-derelict hotels in the company of smug-
glers, pimps, and thieves, painters, bakers, and carriage drivers.
He'd sleep anywhere: on a cheap wet sofa, in putrid stables, or
on the roof of a crumbling apartment building, sharing the rent
with four or five other men. He'd often wander by cinemas, groceries, jewelry shops, or even bars and public squares to sell his
photographs, steal purses, hustle counterfeit liquor, and do a bit
of smuggling, gambling, and pimping as well.

Ismail used to roam to remote corners of the country, then
return with a new look and new clothes and take up work different from what he'd done before. It's possible he was directed
to Mahallet al-Sadriya or to Mahallet Siraj al-Din from the khan
near the Abu Dudu district. Ismail spent six years in this airless,
unlighted khan, a place known to those who saw it from the
outside as a hole or a long labyrinth, opening on a dark space
filled with dirt and putrefying substances. His feet led him there
usually at night, his knife wrapped in a cloth cinched around
his belly. He lay on a mattress as thin as a wooden board and
covered himself with a dirty, colorless blanket, long accustomed

to its pungent smell. Even in this miserable place he was not always safe, as Abboud, the gangster of Siraj al-Din, would push him away and steal his space on the mattress. Ismail placed the mattress on a platform to protect it. This stony elevation served more than one purpose. It was a cupboard to hide his cooking utensils and other valuables, some stolen pornographic photographs he sold, and even some dry bread. It was his dining table during the day and his bedstead at night, and a place to stretch and rest despite the loud snoring of the other occupants. His sleep was often interrupted by the bedbugs gnawing at his skin. He'd scratch at them endlessly and often fall from the mattress onto the ground, where he'd find himself too tired to get up. When he stayed on the floor, he fell victim to cockroaches and rats. He'd bat them away, eyes closed with exhaustion and fatigue.

A rusty iron wire encased a lamp hanging from the ceiling of the khan. It swayed above the head of the Kurdish carrier who was responsible for lighting and extinguishing it. Three other Kurds from Irbil and two from Basra worked as gutter cleaners. They often fought over this miserable lamp before falling off to sleep and filling the room with their moans and snores. Their moaning was sometimes interrupted by the sound of cracking bones, insults, and swearing. When they came back to this place at night shivering, coughing, and spitting, they would sit in a corner and smoke their cheap cigarettes. They usually hunched on their legs, like balls, their teeth crackling from the cold and their behinds numb from the humidity. Sometimes they brought a prostitute, who was even more miserable than they, paler and smellier, and with her hair all stuck together. She'd often be cross-eyed, stammering, lame, or crazy. They'd sleep with her in the same dirty bed, one at a time, laughing like mad, shaking their hands and their pale faces. Once done, they'd shout and jump like monkeys around her, give her money, then one after another go to take a piss.

At dawn Ismail would leave the khan with those failed, broken creatures, exiting from the mangled wooden door of the hotel. They'd all move watchfully, a pack of people who had known nothing but hardship, grief, and moral depravity, swearing, fighting, and stealing. If the police arrested Ismail—for theft or drunkenness or skipping out on his restaurant bill, teasing a girl, or fighting with a prostitute—he would spend the night at the police station, but the inhabitants of the khan would do their duty toward him. They'd treat him with great kindness and generosity, give him money, and bring him food and drink. When he returned to the khan they'd steal his food, drink, and money, and return to their usual selves—dirty, shabbily dressed, hungry, poor, nasty, and most often unemployed. As soon as one of them found work he'd disappear for a while only to return when he lost his job.

Ismail appeared one day in Mahallet al-Sadriya selling pornographic photographs and pictures of Turkish strippers after having lost his municipal job. He went to Mahallet al-Sadriya every day, in fact, for a particular client who was addicted to this type of photograph. No one paid more money for those photographs than Shaul, though the transactions were never straightforward and were concluded only after lengthy haggling and aggravating delays. Still, he always ended up paying the price Ismail was asking. Lately Ismail had been paying more frequent visits to Shaul's shop and was spending more time there. He even received money for some photographs he'd brought from one of the Kurds in the khan. The Kurd was a baggage handler at one of Baghdad's western stations, where he carried the bags of travelers going to Mosul, Basra, or Turkey. Some travelers gave him money, others food, and others gave him dirty photographs to sell. This Kurd was the wealthiest man in the khan. He brought woolen clothes and rare and unique merchandise from Dahuk. He smuggled hash that Ismail ended up getting most of the time, either by raiding his stash at night with Abboud's help, or by buying it for resale to Shaul.

One day Shaul threw his assistant Salim out of his shop. Salim was a Jew who wore his glasses low on his nose and looked over them at people like a hedgehog. He also spoke through his nose. Salim did not like Ismail. He thought he was a swindler who wanted to take his employer's money in exchange for worthless paper photographs. This Saturday morning Salim was thrown from the shop and fell on his face in the street. His glasses fell off his nose. Shaul came out behind him steaming with anger. "You betrayed me, Salim! I made you into a human being. Why did you betray me?"

A couple of days later Shaul was wondering who would replace Salim in the shop. He needed another person, but this time things were different. He was free to choose someone he could mold with his own ideas and principles. His wife had imposed Salim on him because he was a relative of hers. Shaul was convinced that only ideas last, that everything else was futile. If he succeeded in imbuing someone with his ideas and principles he would be able to control and subdue him, if not by making him aware of the social difference that separated them then by their shared ideas. He did not want someone with a set way of thinking, someone who would not acknowledge his debt to him; he wanted someone green, a blank page that he could fill with ideas of his choosing and so induce to think the way he wished. One fine day Ismail entered Shaul's shop with the pornographic photographs deep in the pocket of his shabby, well-worn black jacket. He was disheveled, his hands red from scratching bug bites, and his shirt collar dirty and smelling of cheap arrack. He sat on a clean sofa in a remote corner of the shop filled with shiny new merchandise. He blew his nose in his hand and wore a sad look on his face. Shaul stared at this miserable excuse for a man lurking in the corner. He moved closer until he sat facing him and began to speak softly. Meanwhile Ismail was fingering the smooth photographs in his pocket, trying to judge when might be the right moment to take them out and wondering all the while why Shaul had not asked about them. But Shaul was talking about a totally different subject. He wanted Ismail to understand, he said, that he was a victim of social exploitation, that his adversity was only a temporary situation, and that he would be able to pull him out of it, change him, and provide him with a new appearance. He also told him that nothing in life was permanent, that everything was subject to the vicissitudes of time, a difference in the availability of money, and one's ability to make and spend money. He told him that he, Ismail, would be a different person if he filled his pockets with money, if he worked hard and joined the social order.

Shaul was promising Ismail something concrete, something that would happen to him in this life, something he could touch and feel with his own hands. He told him that his poverty was a historical poverty, not caused by him or his family but the result of History. Ismail was shocked when he heard this and immediately pulled a knife out of his pocket and told him, "Show me History and I will rip out his guts." Shaul smiled and replied, "We have to correct History, not kill it." He uttered those words then smacked his tongue and wet his lips. His eyes gleamed from behind his thick glasses. They were flat, lifeless eyes, moving left and right like plastic beads, and the thick black plastic frames hid his eyebrows.

Shaul's words destroyed the sturdy wall behind which Ismail used to hide. Such serious ideas sent him reeling, though he understood nothing from them except that he could overpower people. He understood only the essence of those words, and, according to Ismail, the essence was that he would get rid of the rags he was wearing, become clean and tidy, and acquire importance in society as others had done. He understood that he'd abandon his unruly life and live an organized one. He'd have to give up the freedom that led him only to misery and enter a life of slavery that would eventually make him a master. Since he had already tried the first kind of life, he was willing with all his heart to try a new one. He was filled with a strong desire to be wealthy and famous, meet clean women, and gain false honor—and the one to provide him with all this was, his savior, Shaul.

Shaul was more drawn to Ismail than the others because he was a strong young man who approached life with all his strength and had spent the early years of his youth experimenting with everything life had to offer, thanks to his social condition. Shaul wanted to build a colony of happiness on earth, and Ismail's wild, dissolute, and lawless way of life was a historical, not an individual, responsibility. History was in fact to blame for Ismail's life of vice and dissolution, for his irresponsible behavior that revolved around the body instead of the mind.

6

This was the first step in cleaning and purifying Ismail, both mentally and physically. Shaul took him first to al-Saada public bath in Bataween, bought him new clothes from the Hisso Brothers' store in al-Rashid Street, and visited the Babet barber to have his hair cut and beard shaved. Ismail gradually learned to live this new life, making the most of the easy, relaxed existence. He saw himself as bigger and more important than he truly was, especially when Shaul helped him take his first steps on the road to the new life. He was puzzled by a life he had not known existed and was seduced by its beautiful, rich, and easy aspects. He visited Shaul's house, a luxurious mansion in eastern Kerrada, close to the gardens overlooking the river. The mansion had its own dense gardens that connected to vast fields and pastures extending as far as the eye could see. Ismail would stare at the huge number of apple, orange, and olive trees on the grounds. There were also palms beautifully displayed in the garden and beyond the fence, and he could see sheep grazing in the distance.

Ismail was awed by the palatial residences he saw on his way to Shaul's mansion. Their roofs were blue, and there were tiles on the facades. He had been walking lazily since he settled in his comfortable life and enjoyed breathing the scent of the fruit around him. When he first arrived at Shaul's mansion he felt lost and uneasy as he gawked at the large house with marble columns, while the sun shone on the stained glass windows and a terrace decorated with expensive baked brick. When he walked across the small bridge near the mansion gate he admired the reflection of the grass on the surface of the water. As soon as the two entered the house through the mahogany gate, Ismail felt the warmth from the heating stove situated in the middle of the beautifully decorated living room. Oak bookshelves stood in each corner, and numerous vases were filled with rare flowers. They both sat on comfortable armchairs covered with soft and valuable Persian rugs. Through the silk curtains Ismail could see the setting sun spreading its red rays over the green fields. In the distance he saw a motionless white fog covering the surface of the river like a thin veil. He felt the rising warmth of the heating stove, and then the smell of the food filled the mansion. A nightingale in a golden cage near the tall window began to sing.

Shaul escorted Ismail to a bedroom on the second floor overlooking the river. Ismail stood transfixed watching the small boats move between the riverbanks. In the distance he saw minarets and the blue roofs of mansions standing along the river. Later on he went downstairs in his cotton bathrobe, warm pajamas, and woolen slippers. He ate dinner, drank tea, and went back to his room, where he slept on a clean, soft, and warm bed. The pillows were stuffed with special feathers, and the blankets were thick Fattah Basha brand. For the first time in his life he felt as if he could fly. He fell into a deep sleep and did not stir until Shaul woke him up at dawn to go to work. Before leaving the house Shaul made sure Ismail brushed his teeth, drank a glass of hot milk, ate a piece of bread, and washed his hands. They were out of the house before sunrise and returned home at the end of the day.

After one week of this regime, Shaul was confident that Ismail was familiar with the merchandise. Ismail began leaving alone in the morning and returning alone in the evening. Shaul went to the store later in the morning and came home in the afternoon. Ismail knew that he was eating and drinking well, but he worked like a donkey and didn't get enough sleep. Early on he began to feel strongly that there was something wrong with this arrangement, something like his own cheating in gambling. Here was Shaul, the man who talked about equality, not performing equal work. He started looking for ways to take advantage of the arrangement because he felt he was being cheated—working the whole day for no salary and being compensated only with room and board—even though he enjoyed a great reputation. He became aware of the shocking contradiction between high society's behavior and the attitude of the noble families on the one hand, and that of the simple poor people on the other. This surprised and upset him and made him anxious, especially after he started to meet important and influential people at receptions at Shaul's house.

Ismail met many of Baghdad's political and literary personalities, who attended these weekly gatherings. Every Thursday and Friday evening Shaul hosted a high tea which was attended by many important personalities, who would gather and discuss serious matters. Among the attendees was Anwar Shaul, Mir Basri, Badr al-Sayyab, and the painter Jamil Hammoudi, one of whose works was hanging on Shaul's wall. There were foreign dignitaries such as Desmond Stewart, the Russian Nicholas Karinsky, and Mary Araminof. The French ambassador, M. Lionel Blanchard and his friend, the painter, Sophie Garso attended those gatherings as well, along with well known personalities such as Rose Khaddouri, Paulina Hassoun, and Amina al-Radi. Dressed in his black suit, Ismail rubbed shoulders with all these luminaries and listened to their complicated discussions. To their animated debates about politics, parties, literature, and the press he could only listen. He understood the essence of what they were saying; the implication was that injustice was widespread and only those people gathering in Shaul's salon were capable of saving the world. During one of those gatherings he witnessed a heated discussion that turned into an exchange of insults between Raphael Batti and another person. Ismail had met Batti before but didn't know his adversary. This made him consider the situation an assault on the house that was hosting the gatherings, and on himself personally. Acting as he did in Khan Abu Dudu, he grabbed a knife from the fruit bowl and attacked the culprit. He missed him but managed to slap him very hard on the face, unaware of the man's cowardice as Batti began shouting and jumping on tables and chairs and running toward the entrance. Some of the guests intervened and tried to stop the fight. When Raphael Batti saw the knife glinting in Ismail's hand close to his face, he fainted. He had never been so close to a threatening knife. His friends revived him by throwing a bucket of water in his face He asked to be carried out of the house, despite Shaul's supplications that he stay. Ismail stood near the stairs, not knowing what to do, but Shaul turned to him and admonished that these were literary disagreements and that he was "in a respectable salon, not Khan Hejjeh."

This hypocrisy and the false feelings of friendship puzzled Ismail. He couldn't understand how these people could strongly disagree with one another and then leave the salon, as if nothing had happened, and pretend to be friends. Their polite words masked a deep dislike, even enmity, for one another. Such a thing would have led to armed fights in the Khan Hejjeh. Dismayed and disbelieving, he watched the guests spend hours criticizing and even insulting a poet, but if he happened to walk into the party they'd receive him like a friend, hugging and kissing him, telling him how much they missed him. This hypocrisy made him uneasy even vis-à-vis Shaul, whose behavior seemed full of contradictions. The rich Shaul, a miser whose main concern was to gather a huge fortune, pretended to build a colony of happiness on earth. He recalled how Shaul had bargained with him long and hard over the price of the pornographic photographs and paid him only after exhausting all possible bargaining tricks. As Ismail examined the beautiful surroundings where he was living, the life of ease and plenty he was enjoying, and the valuable pieces of furniture that filled the house, he wondered whether Shaul had gotten them through such bargaining! Yet Ismail was willing to set aside all his objections to Shaul's behavior and put in their place a naive outlook on matters that would win Shaul over and put his adopter's mind at peace concerning his employee's total acceptance of the concept of inclusive happiness. Deep inside, though, Ismail found it hard to believe Shaul, whom he saw as an irresolute, wavering man who, despite his extreme wealth, bought his pornography at bargain basement prices. How could Ismail then believe that Shaul could build a colony of purity, sacrifice, and happiness? Ismail was unable to resolve this contradictory behavior: the owner of a huge store and a palatial mansion and a believer in the collective right to wealth—why didn't he give his store to the poor and transform his palace into a khan for poor laborers?

Ismail couldn't stand this situation any longer. One day he dared to ask Shaul why he didn't share his store with poor people and put his mansion at the disposal of the miserable workers and porters. The question upset Shaul, who replied angrily, "Would that solve the question of poverty, tell me? The issue of poverty is a historical problem; it was not caused by my mansion. You are wrong in your assessment of things, and he who makes wrong judgments is a devil."

At Shaul's flare-up, Ismail fell totally silent. He hadn't expected his question to provoke such an angry reaction. First of all, because the question was part of 'history,' it became a thorny issue. When he heard the word history, Ismail trembled, fell silent, and avoided interfering in issues having to do with the culprit responsible for the suffering of the universe, whom Shaul accused whenever a problem arose. However he listened carefully to the entire story of the devil that Shaul related to him. The story created even more confusion for Ismail and reinforced his conviction that the measuring process was correct and the devil was right.

The truth of the matter was that Ismail was defending his own interests and happiness and had little interest in the other poor peoples' happiness. He wanted the issues related to his own happiness to remain at the center, which explained his desire to test Shaul's changing personality. He was trying to find a connection between abstract and concrete things. Words and small comments were worthless to him. What counted were palpable things in full form, the things he placed before himself and considered the way Shaul wanted him to. He used to repeat his words only to discover with little effort that culture and the art of speaking are simple. To become a persuasive person it was enough to learn a few phrases, put them in a suitable context, and adopt a certain expression on your face. This matter provoked a certain pleasure in Ismail's emotions and awakened a deep shiver in his soul, one that he kept dormant behind his stiff features.

Ismail Hadoub, this dull, lazy man, this drunkard, had awakened forever. He would never go back to his previous state of mental stagnation. Thanks to Shaul he woke up and was now unstoppable, actively hunting and fishing, seeking as much prey as possible. Ismail was in fact a skilled predator who had come to hunt and chase pleasure with the same acumen he called upon when he was living in poverty and misery. He was poised to sniff out his prey, a gift that poor people had, like dogs that could smell meat from a distance. But was Shaul too naive to notice? Of course not!

Like all wealthy people Shaul thought that he could simulate reconciliation, even a superficial one, with Ismail, like the silky fair skin of a sick woman that hides a devastating illness under its softness. Shaul knew that Ismail coveted money by any means, whether it was acquired wisely or from suspicious sources—insurance money for a road accident, an inheritance, a bankruptcy—it made no difference to him. Shaul was looking for a disciple to exploit, and before satisfying his greed he wanted to tame and examine him under the magnifying glass, the same loupe he used to examine his jewelry. He wanted to downsize him, place him on a flat surface with words, ideas, and expressions, move him a few steps forward and a few steps back, then promote him through his political ideas.

Shaul was convinced that history couldn't be corrected without establishing his happiness colony. Like Jupiter, Shaul was happier whenever he met unhappy people. Ismail was well aware that his time with Shaul was a transition period, because the search for happiness was difficult and the path long, twisted, and profound. On the other hand, he was aware that there was a greater bliss, and that some people changed the concept of happiness, and for them it did not consist of laughter and enjoyment but of tears and sadness. It was a happiness that people sought in order to live a better life. Ismail was made aware that the source of happiness was changeable when Shaul entered the store one day with tears running down his cheeks from lifeless eyes. He was crying over the fate of the hero of a novel he had read the previous night. Ismail had no qualms about imitating Shaul. He cried volubly and beat the table with his hands in a somewhat sarcastic way. He wanted to imitate Shaul's vision of the world in order to set perimeters within which he could act, consistent with the framework Shaul had traced for him. This skilled hunter knew exactly what Shaul wanted from him. He imitated and tricked him, but Shaul did not become aware of his deception until the existentialist philosopher returned to al-Sadriya and Ismail left to follow him. Shaul understood that a human being never sacrificed anything for nothing.

8

Ismail Hadoub was like many other men of letters of modest origin who saw literature and art as a way to gain entry to posh salons and luxurious houses. Art to them was a means to embellish their lives and to help them win over beautiful rich girls. They'd try hard to please such girls, sacrificing their own lives to do so, and when the girls aged they'd look for pleasure with other, younger women. Ismail wanted to use literature to avenge his dignity and build his reputation upon someone else's glory. He wanted to be imposing and rich, to try everything and get everything. He wanted to quench his thirst in life, to arm himself with ideas. He wanted to suck and swallow life, not merely think about it. He wanted to live on other people's accounts, at the expense of merchants, intermediaries, real estate agents, and politicians. Money was the only way to conquer life, and the only way to get money was through literature. But literature required money—checks and cash.

It wasn't an easy equation—not quite as simple as he first thought it would be. Those politicians and merchants who are well trained in the art of exploitation and extortion are not as naive as he thought. They're shrewd and smart. They know how to use others for their own interest and to serve their own plans. They need other people to promote these schemes. They then reward them for their efforts, but the rewards are usually poisoned. Those followers are cheated, and any talk of dignity, honesty, pride, or self-respect is severely punished. The powerful often disapprove of or despise those who use literature to attain wealth. Money is thus in the hands of the wealthy, and getting there was not easy. The wealthy are whimsical and always have the smell of meat on the tips of their fingers. Sometimes they give the morsels to the barking dogs, sometimes to the curs who drool in front of them. Dogs are probably the only ones who know that barking, sniffing, or praising does not pay. This is the power of the rotten creatures over the loose creatures, the power of the masters of pleasure over the weak.

9

Ismail Hadoub had totally changed. His work with Shaul at the store satisfied his vanity and laziness and tamed his violence. He was attracted to the intellectual life, which he encountered through his friendship with Shaul and by living in his house. He knew, however, that Shaul would never forget his protégé's modest origins or the rags he had been wearing before they were thrown into the garbage bin in front of the mansion. Shaul believed that a human being is the product of his conditions and habits. He also believed that an easy life protects a person from his aggressive nature and bestiality, and that it refines and educates him. But he was also aware of the shortcomings in Ismail's knowledge. Ismail finally understood that Shaul was not going to leave him everything after his death as he had initially expected. He understood that Shaul would never willingly bequeath to him the store, the mansion, or the money in his bank account.

In fact Shaul had put everything in the name of his wife, the woman who had run away and cheated on him—rubbing his nose in the mud, as he used to say. The money he held overseas he put in the names of his sons, both of whom lived in London. A few properties were in the name of the Lithuanian mistress, whom he used to meet every summer in Russia. Ismail considered this arrangement stupid and a betrayal of Shaul's principles. He believed that Shaul had the right to punish his despicable adulterous wife and to destroy her as she had destroyed him. Shaul, however, considered human beings to be slaves guided by circumstances that mold them the way the fingers of the hand clear mud of its impurities. Shaul didn't believe in Ismail's genius. He never forgot that no matter how much he changed he would remain a peddler of pornographic photographs, and he would not forget that it was Shaul who had pulled him out of his misery and made something of him. Ismail had no right to the wealth that Shaul had acquired through his efforts and a life of struggle. Ismail's hopes to inherit Shaul's money dissipated, and the dreams he enjoyed his first night on the comfortable bed in his benefactor's mansion turned into a nightmare on his last day there.

Ismail became unequivocally aware that happiness was a concrete matter, not a theoretical one. He believed that money was to be spent, not accumulated and saved, the same way the eyes could not look at the glittering sight of gold without tearing and a man could not view a woman without desiring her. He realized that there was another kind of life, other than the miserable, dry, and empty life of culture provided by Shaul. His life with Shaul was joyless. He was deprived of women, drinking, and general hell-raising. He was naturally inclined toward the pleasures of life. His heart melted before succulent, intoxicating things and was deeply moved by the pursuit of shiny, velvety objects that hid, under their coarseness, tenderness, sex, and drugs. Those were the things Ismail believed in, loved, and instinctively sought out. Ismail wanted to attain wealth, receive admiration, and enjoy prestige at any price. He wanted to reach the summit, to enter the abode of pleasure. He wanted concrete matters, not those things that only the mind could reach. He was no longer satisfied simply to fill his stomach; he had gotten used to better things. He was getting ready to move to the next level, and he knew that this would not happen with Shaul's help. First, Ismail mentally dismissed his benefactor and then began searching for someone else. And that was Abd al-Rahman.

10

Ismail Hadoub left Shaul to join Abd al-Rahman. In this move Ismail adopted the methods of a hunter, one who wants to catch life with philosophy rather than hunt philosophy through life. He followed Abd al-Rahman because, unlike Shaul, he talked about life in a practical and appealing way, with precision, elegance, and humor. Shaul lacked all those attributes and so did his culture. Abd al-Rahman's philosophy was more attractive because existentialism was clearer than Marxism. For example, whenever Abd al-Rahman said "nihilism" it meant that he wanted to get drunk, and whenever he said "freedom" he was planning on sleeping with a woman, and "commitment" meant an appointment at a bar or nightclub. This is how Ismail explained Abd al-Rahman's philosophy to one of his new friends at the Coronet bookstore.

Abd al-Rahman's philosophy contained enjoyable things, while Shaul's happiness colony required struggle and fighting. One could struggle and possibly die without ever attaining that stage; what kind of paradise was this? In immediate taste and gratification Ismail found a rich interpretation of life. He cringed at delayed enjoyments.

Ismail's escape from Shaul was first met with a smile from the philosopher, but later he welcomed him without reservations. He reacted to Shaul's anger by supporting Ismail, who had opted for freedom, and because, as Abd al-Rahman explained to his disciple, freedom is a commitment. Ismail on the other hand considered his personal choice an echo of lingering memories. He stood before the philosopher and told him that he had been a philosopher since infancy. When his words were reported to Shaul, his former benefactor commented sarcastically, "Do you really believe that this ass was wrapped in a proper layette like normal human beings? He's a bastard. His prostitute mother abandoned him in a stream."

Ismail left Shaul propelled by a stubborn idea: he was seeking love, sex, alcohol, and other pleasures. As for Abd al-Rahman, he did not see any dramatic aspect to Ismail's decision. He considered it a normal inclination on the part of all human beings to indulge in life's pleasures. It was obvious that the fulfillment of that inclination required spending time in cafés and at philosophical nights of debauchery at the Grief Adab nightclub. In brief, it was a life of drinking, sex, and disregard for all traditions.

11

Rumors and gossip surrounded Ismail Hadoub's departure from Shaul to join Abd al-Rahman, the philosopher of al-Sadriya. The whisperings drove Shaul crazy and pushed him to violent rages. He shouted threats against Ismail at the top of his lungs. His words of abuse were heard by passersby, who were amused by his pronunciation of *r* as *gh* and his threatened reprisals against

Ismail. The scene was an entertainment for the scoundrels of al-Sadriya, who laughed and joked at Shaul's expense, which only fueled his fits of anger. Some of the salesmen in the neighborhood felt sorry for him and intervened. They chased away the scoundrels and beat their donkeys, provoking noisy quarrels with the fruit sellers, butchers, sheep herders, pottery makers, and china merchants. Those quarrels sometimes caused Shaul to shake violently and fall to the ground.

12

Abd al-Rahman crossed al-Matajer Street in al-Sadriya souk every day at noon, carrying an umbrella dripping with rain water and wearing a black raincoat. He shivered in the cold and advanced with uncertain steps, while his mother-of-pearl-encrusted pipe hung from his mouth.

Ismail found the philosopher's personality very attractive because he was the personification of laziness, carelessness, and moral degradation. He explained every immoral action as a natural inclination dormant in every person's conscience. Ismail considered philosophy more dangerous than theoretical conversation about the happiness colony.

13

Abd al-Rahman and Ismail often staggered home drunk after a night of low pleasures at a nightclub. When they reached the top of the street, they slowed their pace until they reached Shaul's shop, then vomited in front of the door, wiped their mouths with their sleeves, and ran off. Shaul used to run after them brandishing a broomstick, but they always managed to disappear around the corner of the street as quickly as exploding sticks of dynamite.

Sometimes the two men would stop at the end of the street, where there was an abundance of bordellos with long queues of gentlemen waiting to pull down their elegant pants. Some of the women in question appeared in corsets, while others poured their bath water at the thresholds of their rooms, laughing noisily.

14

Abd al-Rahman and Ismail went out daily, either in a taxi, or a carriage drawn by two gray horses for a fare not more than one dirham. They liked to use a carriage to take them from the nightclub near the Roxy cinema to King Ghazi Street and back. Each would sit in a corner of the carriage as they rode through the crowded streets of the residential areas, between the heavily scented eucalyptus trees, talking with the driver about bootleg arrack and imported whiskey. The narrow streets surrounding them were filled with women in black abayas, imitation jewelry shining under their sleeves. When the carriage reached Zubayda Square, it made its way with great difficulty, as it was hampered by throngs of people, especially children playing in the streets. Women sat on the thresholds of their quarters or peered from their half-open windows; others sat on the roofs. The carriage driver, who wore a scarf tied over his head and whipped the horses' flanks, quarreled with the grocers, silk merchants, and rabble who lined the street before he took Abd al-Rahman and Ismail to Grief Adab, where Dalal Masabni was waiting for them.

15

Dalal Masabni was the most famous dancer of her time. She was born in Baghdad of a Lebanese mother named Aida Qastali and an Iraqi father. The mother was known for her impetuosity and adventures, but the father's identity was unknown. Some believed that he was a tradesman of great repute in Mosul and was hiding in Baghdad under the false name of Abd al-Hamid al-Hashemi. After the departure of his wife and his fifteen-year-old daughter to Lebanon, he left the house he had rented for them and went to Iran. There, traces of him disappeared forever. Aida didn't like living in Beirut, so a year later she went to America with a man she had met in one of the gambling halls. She placed her daughter Dalal in the care of a famous drug trafficker who called himself Sami al-Khouri. He was none other than the well-known drug kingpin who was featured on the pages of the international press in the sixties and who gave Interpol a run for its money with his capers and large-scale trafficking. He had a special inclination for beautiful women and finally fell in love with the French singer Maria Vincent, whom he met at the Cordon Bleu nightclub in Istanbul.

The fact is that Dalal had met Sami on al-Hamra Street in Ras Beirut long before he had become famous. She was fifteen years old and had just arrived with her mother. It was Samira Shuwayri, Beirut's most famous belle at the time, who introduced her to Sami. Despite her youth, Dalal worked as a professional dancer at the Masabni nightclub. She soon left her job at the club to live in the luxurious apartment that Sami owned in the Roche. Her long blond hair, thin figure, narrow waist, and calm gaze attracted much attention. All of Beirut was talking about the new girl who went riding around with the drug dealer in his Cadillac and ate dinner with him at the Cave restaurant. They used to sit in a dark corner drinking champagne. After midnight they'd go to the casino to gamble. She stood near him holding two glasses of whiskey, one for her and one for him. She gave his whiskey to him to drink one sip at a time, still holding the glass. Two years later Dalal's photograph appeared on the front page of the local Lebanese papers, and other Arab newspapers as well, standing close to Sami after he was caught in the largest-ever hashish smuggling operation to Cairo.

Dalal was arrested at the Regent Hotel in Cairo. She was a nervous wreck, trying to control her shakes with a cigarette and blowing the smoke into the air. She was anxiously watching the door when two men from the Egyptian secret service knocked. They asked whether she was Dalal and after she confidently acknowledged her identity, she left with them. The servants and hotel employees watched her being led to a large black Mercedes in front of the hotel, that drove off at a high speed.

Dalal sat before the prosecutor on a comfortable chair. His desk had an inkwell, pencils, and a small case that she recognized as Sami's. She faced the heavyset interrogator, who asked her boldly but politely about the drugs that Sami had smuggled into Cairo, all the while staring into her beautiful sad eyes. She did not reply. Soon Sami was brought in, and when she saw him, she stood up to hug him. He was quick to inform the police that she had had nothing to do with the drugs and served only as a cover. Dalal looked at him affectionately, but he covered his face with his hands without saying a word.

After an intensive investigation the prosecutor could not implicate her and was forced to release her. She was sent back to Beirut, and Sami was condemned to two years in an Egyptian prison. Dalal returned to their apartment in Beirut to wait for her lover, and rarely went out. She was attended by a Greek maid whom Sami trusted fully. As she spent the days recalling the sad moments of his arrest and the good times they had spent together, the old maid informed her that it was the first time that he had been caught and that it had happened because he feared for her life. Sami's willingness to sacrifice himself for her strengthened her love and attachment to him.

One day she learned from the maid that Sami had returned to Beirut. She waited for him at the apartment, but he did not show up that day or the days following. His friends asked her to be discreet because he feared for her life. She became suspicious, especially when she learned that he had traveled to Istanbul for a new deal. She waited for him again, until months later she heard that he had married the French singer Maria Vincent. That was the last she heard of him until one day a friend of his brought her a packet of money with a message from Sami, informing her of his marriage to the French singer and freeing her from any commitment.

Dalal returned to the same nightclub where she had met Sami and joined a group of belly dancers performing there. She performed with them for some time but was soon fed up with this exhausting job. She couldn't compete with professional dancers who had trained in the top dance studios and with the best teachers in Beirut and Cairo. She decided to return to Baghdad and, with the money the smuggler had left her, she opened the Grief Adab. It did not take long for her to become well known throughout the city, especially after the philosopher became one of her customers. This connection gave her a reputation as a patron of writers and culture. She had a table permanently reserved for Abd al-Rahman with a sign that read "reserved for the philosopher."

17

The philosopher was excited by Dalal's voluptuous red lips, which held her white cigarette tightly. The smoke she was in the habit of blowing in his face smelled of alcohol and her favorite perfume. Knowing her was liberating and tickled him provocatively, especially when her body quivered left and right and she chewed gum. He was very attached to her because of the sense of freedom he felt with her—no jealousy and no moral or social responsibility. With her he was not concerned with values especially those related to honor. Dalal had the capacity to free him of responsibility, and this freedom was the reason he was so attached to her. He was well aware that she had known many men before him and that she would know many after him, but she was fair, balanced, and had common sense. In a distorted kind of way, she was philosophical.

Dalal used to receive an English friend in her room. She claimed he was giving her English lessons, but she always sent him away the moment the philosopher stepped inside the nightclub. She used to walk her English friend to the door and bid him a polite and subtle adieu, then welcome the philosopher at the same door and with the same good manners, maintaining a balance in her relationships with both of them. Neither felt that she was giving the other more importance, as she divided her attention equally between the two. She demonstrated great skill in this ceremonial sending of one friend away and welcoming of the other.

When she finished her dance, she sat at the philosopher's table to enjoy his and Ismail's company. Sometimes she accepted other customers' invitations to spend time at their tables, but she only did that reluctantly. She felt superior to the other customers, who knew nothing about philosophy. She enjoyed the company of her peers, those with the same intellectual interests. Abd al-Rahman didn't mind sharing her with the others. He didn't want her to himself because he did not want to feel responsible for her. He wanted her to belong to everyone in order to rid himself of any sense of jealousy, for the feeling of jealousy was not philosophical. Abd al-Rahman's attitude puzzled Ismail, whose tribal and primitive values considered it a kind of insult. He couldn't understand that the dancer was the philosopher's mistress and yet he sat with others. Abd al-Rahman used to answer such smug oriental ideas with a philosophical image, "You will not become a true existentialist unless you get rid of this oriental jealousy."

"But she is your friend," Ismail would counter, to which Abd al-Rahman responded, "Yes, my friend, but it does not mean that I should become jealous."

To convince his friend, Abd al-Rahman related an incident that involved Jean Paul Sartre and was witnessed by Abd al-Rahman in person, "Once I was visiting my friend Sartre, and Simone was present—I mean Simone de Beauvoir, of course. Naturally, there were other philosophers such as Merleau Ponty and Gabriel Marcel there as well. We were drinking heavily and feeling nauseated. In other words it was a little invitation to experience nausea in Sartre's apartment. I was talking with my friend Sartre about some fundamental differences between us and suggested changes to include in his philosophy. He agreed with me on every single word I said and every single letter, in other words he agreed with me all the way."

Ismail shouted, "Isn't that great!"

The philosopher went on as he continued to drink his whiskey and blow smoke in his companion's face. "Simone had disappeared and while Sartre was looking for his pencil case he wanted to ask her whether she had it or had seen it. We couldn't find it anywhere in the house. The only place we had not searched was Simone's bedroom."

Ismail, shocked, interrupted him and asked whether they had entered her bedroom.

"Yes, we did, and we found her lying on the bed with her skirt pulled up, and Gabriel Petrovitekch was on top of her."

"Who's he?" inquired Ismail.

Abd al-Rahman explained, "He's a Russian existentialist. He uses the pen name Midanoviski."

Aghast, Ismail took a deep breath, raised his eyebrows as if he had just recovered from his drunkenness, and asked, "What did Sartre do?"

"Nothing, nothing," explained Abd al-Rahman, hesitantly. "He told her, I am sorry darling, I didn't mean to disturb you."

Ismail Hadoub was stunned; his jaw dropped, and his eyes shone from the effects of alcohol and surprise. The story disturbed him deeply; he was angry and disgusted. Until then he had had a great respect for Simone de Beauvoir and had never heard such anecdotes about her. Yet he did not want to give up his friendship with the philosopher who went to France and witnessed existentialism with his own eyes, unlike any other Iraqi. Books, no matter how accurate they are, cannot transmit ideas as faithfully as an eyewitness. Abd al-Rahman had personally witnessed existentialism. He had touched it, felt it, and stuck to it like no one else, unlike those who did not see it but dreamt of it and imagined it.

Abd al-Rahman stood apart from other existentialists in the country. A huge gap separated him from them, for there is a difference between the one who has known something, experienced it, and endured it, and the one who has only imagined it. Abd al-Rahman must have truly known existentialism, in flesh and blood, like no one else.

Ismail suddenly had an idea. He began acting on it the afternoon following the one he had spent with the al-Sadriya philosopher at Grief Adab. He was often absent from the philosopher's company, joining him occasionally in the evenings at the café or at Dalal Masabni's nightclub. He claimed to be working at the *Abnaa al-zaman* newspaper and told the philosopher that Salim Malkun had asked him to write a piece about existentialism and Sartre in reply to an article by Suhail Idris, the distorter.

Abd al-Rahman objected to Suhail Idris's tendency to combine nationalism and existentialism, an approach that seemed rather comical to him. He made fun of the author and mocked him loudly every time someone called Idris a nationalist. He didn't believe that politics or ideology played a part in existentialism. Whenever Shaul mentioned that Sartre wrote political articles, Abd al-Rahman poked fun at him and all those who shared that opinion. He argued that the poor quality of the

Arabic translations gave the false impression that Sartre's writings had a political content. Abd al-Rahman not only disliked politics, he despised it. He recoiled from those who practiced politics and those who discussed it. He considered existentialism a mere feeling of nausea, a permanent nausea provoked by everything political, social, moral, and life-related.

Ismail's absences became more frequent, and he rarely met with the philosopher, a big change from the past when he was with him almost always and everywhere. He described his absences as a Sartrian and existential commitment, a responsibility, yet not a philosophical responsibility of the kind Suhail Idris pretended to have, but an existential responsibility. Abd al-Rahman provided excuses and justifications for Ismail's absences and never asked about him. All that concerned the philosopher was Ismail's response to Suhail Idris. The truth of the matter is that Abd al-Rahman hated One-Eyed Jaseb's attacks on Idris because they were aimed at an existentialist, even though Abd al-Rahman disagreed with Idris. He used to ask the public at the café, "Did Sartre approve of Gabriel Marcel?" and everyone would reply in one voice, "No."

Ismail's explanation for his absences couldn't be further from the truth. He was not going to *Abnaa al-zaman* every day as he had told his friend the philosopher and as was confirmed by many of al-Sadriya's inhabitants. The journal's editor, Salim Malkun, was not a stupid man and would never have assigned to Ismail the responsibility of replying to the Arab World's then most famous existentialist. He could not put himself in such an embarrassing position, as he knew very well Ismail's weak style, his inability to write without mistakes, and his obscure, ridiculous ideas. A typical passage might read as follows: "Existentialism—what is existentialism? In reality it is an existential nausea, a type of nausea that Sartre, the father of the wonderful existential nausea, taught us. He wrote the novel *Nausea* in one month, as confirmed by the philosopher of al-Sadriya, who saw him in person in Paris and is married to his cousin." The article would then be filled with a series of insults against all those who criticize existentialism. The names of Shaul and One-Eyed Jaseb were usually among them.

There was no way a respectable newspaper like *Abnaa al-zaman* could publish such rubbish. When Ismail used to read them to Abd al-Rahman in the presence of the dancer Badi'a, in the midst of the hubbub created by the singers and drunks, the shouting of the prostitutes, the swearing, the overturned chairs, and the rushing servers, Badi'a would pulse with admiration for this virile man. Abd al-Rahman felt the articles were missing something but was not able to pinpoint what.

Abd al-Rahman found excuses for Ismail's repeated absences, which soon became established fact. He was the only one to believe Ismail's excuses and accepted that he was on an existential mission. Badi'a had her doubts when she noticed Ismail's lack of interest in Wazzeh, one of the prostitutes. She tried to draw the philosopher's attention to Ismail's absences, but it was in vain. He was convinced that Ismail was on an existential mission, a great undertaking, even though it con-sisted of writing meaningless articles—but then again life is meaningless. As long as Ismail did not claim to be a philoso-pher like him, he would tolerate his absences and expect him to defend the philosopher's den and shut up One-Eyed Jaseb, Shaul, and others.

I learned from more than one source in Mahallet al-Sadriya that Ismail paid frequent visits to the philosopher's house dur-ing his absence. He established a relationship with his wife, whom Ismail truly believed to be Sartre's cousin. He was con-vinced that as long as he could lie on the cousin of Sartre, the greatest French philosopher, it was as if he had slept with the whole of France.

18

A poor vagabond like Ismail had nothing but his virility to boast about, something that could attract a Frenchwoman who had had no sexual relations with her husband since they mutually lost their attraction to one another.

Every evening he would saunter down Mahallet Abu Dudu, go past the Christian quarter, then the convent courtyard, and finally to the Jewish quarter. He wandered into al-Sadriya in front of the roosters' cage, listening to the calls of the fruit vendors and watching the women wrapped in their abayas and those sporting the latest hairstyles.

Shaul knew very well where Ismail went, so did One-Eyed Jaseb as he shouted praise for the apples he sold on his cart, and Hamdiya who sold her merchandise at the souk. Even Dr. Simon Bahlawan knew where Ismail Hadoub went in the morning and sometimes in the evening, leaving only a half hour before the husband's return.

The philosopher, on the other hand, continued visiting his mistress openly each night and experiencing his usual nausea.

19

Existentialism was the philosophy of choice for Iraqi intellectuals in the sixties, which explains why the arrival of the philosopher to Mahallet al-Sadriya was considered the greatest event of that decade; his presence filled a huge philosophical gap. The intellectuals of the time could not wait forever, for the appearance of a new major philosophy or a philosophical interpretation of an existing major philosophy. They were eagerly anticipating the arrival of such a historical event and were, according to numerous sources, lost in pseudo-philosophies.

It was in this condition of confusion and loss that Abd al-Rahman, son of Mr. Shawkat and the greatest philosophical mind of his time, appeared on the scene. Without him they would not have been able to put a radical end to this complex philosophical problem. He brought them an authentic philosophy, not a false one, a unique philosophy that was not a mere copy of French existentialism, or a passive artificial interpretation, but a creative Arabic interpretation of it. This all happened thanks to Abd al-Rahman's constructive efforts in formulating and establishing this philosophy and his pushing it onto a path that its founder, M. Jean-Paul Sartre, would never have thought possible.

20

Following a philosopher differs from following a follower of philosophy. Abd al-Rahman was a philosopher; therefore, being his follower was not like being Suhail Idris, a follower of philosophy. With such a concept it is understandable that Abd al-Rahman was able to gather a large number of followers around him in the sixties.

Abd al-Rahman's withdrawal from upper-class society and the soirées of noble families essentially forced him to seek his public in the streets and to lower his standards in order to reach his followers. Being wealthy, handsome, young, and elegant gave him independence and power and moved him in the direction of instinctive pleasures. He was able to associate with those less fortunate than himself, such as Ismail Hadoub, and such actions provided proof of his correctness and humility. Ismail Hadoub, on the other hand, considered the matter a privilege for himself and an appreciation of his genius, which made up for his modest background. This motivated him to become intimately attached to the al-Sadriya philosopher. He spent wonderful days with him, walking behind him, carrying a notebook and a golden pen, writing down the valuable words uttered by the philosopher.

On a cold January day, as it was raining heavily in Baghdad, Ismail stood in front of a café where the philosopher was sipping coffee. He wore nothing but a woolen sweater that Shaul had given him when he was working in his store. He was shivering from the cold, and as soon as Abd al-Rahman saw him he took off his black woolen coat and placed it on Ismail's shoulders. "You represent to me what Simone de Beauvoir represented to Sartre," he said. The public in the café heard those words and began spreading them everywhere. It became known that the philosopher took good care of his followers. He shaped them and made sacrifices for their sake.

People were somewhat surprised by the intimate friendship between the two men. They were surprised by the existential image that conveyed truly the humanitarian side of this goodhearted existentialist, this nauseated person, this bright, energetic Sartrian who surpassed Sartre himself. Four years later Ismail Hadoub betrayed Abd al-Rahman and slept with his French wife. The scandal was known all over the country. Abd al-Rahman died, a homicide or suicide, and Sartre's cousin returned to her country. Iraqi intellectuals everywhere declared that Sartre was embarrassed by the scandal. All that remained of Abd al-Rahman was the black coat on Ismail's shoulders.

21

When the existential philosopher had lost his way in the metropolis of existentialism and before he had found the house he was looking for in Gay-Lussac Street, he encountered his destiny standing on the sidewalk wearing a dark red suit, a woolen coat, and a simple woolen hat This is where he met Germaine, the woman he later married, and through her he espoused a whole nation.

Before he met Germaine, however, he had a painful and sentimental experience with a young woman who was working as a waitress in the Café de Flore in Saint Germain. It was a story of a tortured love. She was, in a way, the miracle that mended a rift in the philosopher's life. Unbeknownst to her she was the one who saved him from a horrible fate that would have led him into a wasteland. While Germaine took him to an environment of philosophy and unbelievable existential scenes, the Café de Flore waitress brought bitterness, confusion, emptiness, and sorrow to his life.

The philosopher was enamored of the waitress the moment he set eyes on her round and firm, protruding breasts, visible through the opening in her shirt. He imagined himself talking frankly to her about his feelings in order to stop the erupting volcano in his life. It was only his cowardice that stopped him and kept him away from these golden mountains that held him prisoner by their sweetness and attraction. Feeling helpless, he used to sit at a table, drinking beer or a cup of hot tea, his pipe lying on the table near *Le Monde* or one of Sartre's books, watching her. He would sit there in silence, giving the impression of being a thinker who was pondering a wild and adventurous life. Deep inside him there was nothing but emptiness and sexual visions floating freely each time the waitress bent over to serve a table or toyed with the cross between her breasts.

One day she bent over his table to clean an ashtray and remove an empty beer glass. His eyes fell on the rounded shape of her full breasts that were swelling beneath her white woolen sweater. She asked him what he was thinking about. Her question was God-sent, as he had long wanted to draw her attention to his superior intellect so that he might dazzle her with his philosophy and ability to penetrate the open horizons of his being, but he had not known how to do it. She took him by surprise. He felt a little nervous but managed to smile at her as his heart rate rose significantly and his voice rattled in his throat. He replied spontaneously and philosophically, "I have been thinking about

Sartre's opinion of women. He said that they could not do without men." The pipe was shaking in his hand, his heart was beating, and his lips were trembling. The waitress laughed quietly, pushed back an unruly lock of blond hair hiding her blue eyes, winked at him and said, "Do you really need Sartre's head to know this?"

Her reply came as a surprise to him, such a totally and unexpectedly straightforward and hurtful answer, a little mocking even. He had expected her to open her mouth and say, in amazement, "Oh! Are you a philosopher?" Then the wheel of his fortune would have turned, moving from sadness to happiness. She would have stood on the threshold of a huge change that would have led them to an almost total melding. She would have learned to bring to light the hidden, mysterious, and incomplete side of her personality. Through his continuous efforts to express his secret self, she would have discovered the secret lying dormant in his soul. It was obvious that something bothered him and he needed a romantic relationship that would guide him to important people and those strongly biased in favor of their own ideas. But the answer he received was shattering and thus reduced him to shards scattered across the floor. He turned extremely pale as she turned her back and disappeared behind a door. All that remained in his imagination was the memory of her thighs, softly shaking. With trembling hands and grinding teeth he gathered his newspapers, books, stuffed pipe, and eyeglasses and left the café, catching the last breath of his failure.

22

He angrily pushed open his apartment door and threw himself on the bed, where he remained for a very long time. He felt defeated, as if he had been involved in a scandal. He pounded the pillow with his fists, saying, "It is my fault. If I weren't so stupid I wouldn't have said what I said. She embarrassed me. She should have been nicer to me."

He felt as though his head was cloven in two and each half offered a solution—not a guaranteed solution but at least a solution. He felt torn, crushed, victimized. It was at that moment that he became aware of his tragic fate, the way he had in Baghdad with Nadia Khaddouri. It happened at a difficult period in his life, a time when he felt rejected, odd, and dismayed. He had to choose a way to find the courage to confront the savage monster roaming loose within him. He did so, but not until the following day.

23

At noon the following day, in rainy autumnal weather, Abd al-Rahman left his apartment in a hurry. He welcomed the refreshing breeze that hit his face and moved through his hair. He kept his hands in his raincoat pockets and lowered his hat on his forehead. He kept his eyes on the road in an effort to avoid walking in the puddles and headed toward Saint Michel to meet an Iraqi friend who had been living in Paris for many years.

The grass in the Jardin du Luxembourg was wet and fragrant, the streets were slick with rain, the buildings had been washed, and the trees revealed their dark green color. Abd al-Rahman met Ahmad near a telephone booth at the corner of the street. They walked toward Rue Monsieur le Prince in silence. Abd al-Rahman's facial expression revealed his disturbed state of mind. He felt humiliated and disappointed and he wanted his friend's advice on what his next step with the waitress should be, while recognizing his own gaucherie.

"I want to make a plan," he told his friend angrily, "I want her to regret what she said to me. I want to change her mind." Ahmad asked his friend for a cigarette. It was obvious from his reaction that he was used to the way the philosopher spoke. He asked whether there were reasons for his interest in her, to which Abd al-Rahman responded, "I've had enough of prostitutes, that's why. Do you understand?" Ahmad realized that the philosopher couldn't resist his physical attraction to that woman. He knew that he wouldn't let go before he slept with her, though he was not in love with her. He was a jealous man but unable to make a decision.

Abd al-Rahman asked his friend if he had found out anything about her. "Yes," said Ahmad, "I've learned some important things about her."

"Tell me," said the philosopher.

Ahmad filled him in. "I learned that she has an Algerian friend named Si Muammar." Abd al-Rahman stopped suddenly in the middle of the street. A cigarette dangling from his lips, he asked, "Is that so?" Ahmad nodded and added with a relaxed smile, "It is true, and I can get to know him."

"What about me?" asked Abd al-Rahman, with a strange look. Ahmad explained his plan, "Of course, of course, I'll get to know him for your sake."

The prospect of reaching her at any price was a torture for Abd al-Rahman. It took him back to his bestial nature, where instinct dictated his behavior. He wanted her by all means, at any price, whether it required begging, raping, killing, betraying, or torturing her. He left Ahmad near the newspaper stand and went to satisfy the call of nature in the *pissoir* at the end of Odeon Street. Peeing brought a sense of comfort and relaxation, and his mind fixed on the sight of the crumbling wall of an old church and a flock of pigeons flying from the roof of a building nearby. He rejoined his friend, feeling relieved and even a bit elated. The sky began to clear, and the sun was breaking through the clouds, warming up the puddles in the streets. Everything around him looked beautiful: the facades of buildings, the flowers in the squares, the *cafés trottoires* with their colorful parasols, the vegetable market, and the newspaper kiosks. His anxiety was washed away, and he recovered his old sense of comfort. He watched with joy as the streets came to life around him. Saint-Germain-des-Prés stretched in front of him like a velvet carpet. He did not mind the blowing horns, the blinking red lights of the street bars, or the rush of pedestrians that filled the place this time of day. Women dressed in their going-out clothes emerged from side streets smoking cigarettes, their lips colored bright red with lipstick. He shouted in Ahmad's face, "I'll get to know her through Si Muammar, won't I?"

"Certainly," replied Ahmad.

24

The philosopher was convinced that if he could talk to her even through her friend, he could win her over. He wasn't short on means to court her, but he didn't know the path to her heart. Once she was with him he could employ his many unfailing methods: a promenade at sunset over the bridge crossing an icy river, being alone with her in a room filled with the sound of music and the smell of coffee, together watching ducks floating on a pond. He would rush her with a list of terms that revealed complex values such as: 'existence,' 'eternity,' 'time,' 'absurdity,' and 'nausea.' She would undoubtedly be seduced by this oriental philosopher who had come to Paris equipped with a powerful philosophy and who had memorized the entire philosophical lexicon.

Her own compatriots lacked this quality, and what does a waitress wish for more than to become friends with a philosopher? She'll regret having made fun of him that one time in the past. She will kneel at his feet and admit her ignorance. Once she learns that he is the philosopher's student and he himself is a philosopher, she'll want to get close to him, love him, and discover his inner force that she once almost inadvertently destroyed. Abd al-Rahman reflected aloud, "Who is this Algerian compared to me!"

"No one" said Ahmad.

The philosopher wondered, puzzled "Why did she befriend him then?"

Ahmad offered, "Maybe because he keeps her."

This was no challenge to the philosopher, who explained his plan, "If this is the case, I'll take her out of the Café de Flore. I'll even buy the café for her."

There was only one other thing the philosopher wanted to inquire about, but he was a little embarrassed to ask. He took his hands out of his pockets, adjusted his glasses and walked gracefully, showing off his youthful body. He considered those characteristics central to his relationship with women. Then asked, "Is this Si Muammar handsome?"

Ahmad laughed loudly. "No, not at all. I saw him a few times in the Latin Quarter. His face looks like a cognac bottle."

This response liberated Abd al-Rahman, who started laughing loudly. His eyes twinkled, and he felt joyful and relieved. His heart was beating fast, and his cheeks were hot from emotion. He asked Ahmad, "Is he as elegant as I am?"

"That would be impossible. He wears rags, like the Paris clochards. People say he is a drug addict and spends his time with users, pickpockets, and all the lazy guys." Abd al-Rahman shouted joyfully, "That's great!"

The philosopher adopted an affected walk, he was proud of his virility, his youth, his strength, and he made fun of effeminate young Frenchmen. The two friends stopped at a nearby café and were served by a plump waitress wearing country clothes under her red sweater. Her smile revealed a gold tooth. They ordered two beers. The place had a nostalgic ambiance, and Abd al-Rahman felt an inclination for jokes, wisdom, and lust

When Ahmad broached the subject, he was certain of the effect his words would have on his friend. He said, "There's only one thing." Abd al-Rahman asked what it was. Ahmad explained, "People say he is an existentialist."

"Existentialist!" echoed Abd al-Rahman. He put down the glass of beer he had begun to drink. Ahmad's revelation hit the philosopher like a thunderbolt. After a short silence he wondered, "Is it true, does he understand existentialism? How?" Ahmad wore a smile of compassion and looked for a way to lessen the shock on his friend. He felt the concern of the philosopher, his anxiety. "I don't know much. They say he holds long discussions and describes himself as an existentialist."

Abd al-Rahman was seriously worried. His expression betrayed deep hatred for this Algerian, but he was not crushed. He wet his dry lips with sips of beer. The philosopher was not convinced that Si Muammar could do anything except memorize a dictionary of existentialist terms. Whatever the existentialism of this man with the cognac-bottle-shaped face, it would be easy for Abd al-Rahman to best him, or so he thought. As soon as they met face-to-face he would inundate him with a series of philosophical definitions, even disconnected ones, then confuse him, surprise him, and overpower him verbally. Si Muammar wouldn't be able to say a word.

The surprise would muzzle him. The waitress of Café de Flore would be stunned and overjoyed. She'd look at Abd al-Rahman with affectionate eyes, rush to his side, and tell him, "You are truly a philosopher, your abstruse words are magical!" She'd recognize the difference between a philosopher and a clochard, a true philosopher and an imposter. She would notice for the first time the richness of his soul, his calm, and poise. She would fall in love with his dreamy eyes, which resembled the eyes of prophets. She would listen to his prophetic voice, the voice of a messenger. She would become aware of his sensual side, his love of food, and earthly pleasures. She would note his handsome appearance, his lust, his sexual proclivities, and his philosophical personality.

"What more could a waitress want?" he shouted and hit the table with his hand, scaring his friend, whose neck had sunk into his coat. Ahmad regained his self-control quickly and said, "Don't think of her as your significant other, yet."

Teary-eyed, his cheeks burning red from emotion and the heat of love, Abd al-Rahman made a solemn declaration, "I will make her my significant other, believe me. I'll be her gift." Ahmad commented on his friend's words saying, "This is real generosity. You are truly generous." He resumed drinking his beer.

25

Ahmad managed to convince the philosopher of the soundness of his ideas. He was a gifted talker and persuasive speaker who used flattery to accomplish his aims and never defied his friend. His heavy drinking helped endear him to people. It gave him a hoarse voice that was comforting and friendly. His conversation was histrionic, but his tone was warm and reassuring. Presented in an agreeable way, his most insignificant ideas acquired importance.

The philosopher, on the other hand, was a practical man, and alcohol emboldened him. He asked Ahmad whether the meeting with the waitress would be easy, and Ahmad reassured him it would be. The philosopher was convinced of his ability to assert himself and his power over others. He held tight to this imaginary victory out of need for a relationship, and he was ready to conquer the waitress at Café de Flore to show her a pure image of himself, an unadulterated image free of scandal and sarcasm. He intended to reach his target by crushing his debaters and was intent on revenge to expunge the humiliation he had endured at her hands. He was bent on revenge at any cost to advance the image of a very proud man and to conceal his delicate, wounded soul.

Abd al-Rahman thought to himself, "Si Muammar will swallow the bait. Our friendship will be a mere device to reach the waitress of Café de Flore."

He laughed noisily, and the whiskey vapors escaped from his mouth. He didn't feel guilty, because he didn't have a normal conscience. He had a philosopher's conscience, a conscience that philosophy had killed. He didn't think like normal human beings, who are considerate of others. His tyranny overpowered any benign feelings he had. He wanted to impose his will on those around him, and he found great pleasure in using his might. Thinking aloud he said, "No, he'll not be my friend," then fell silent.

"Of course not," agreed Ahmad.

Abd al-Rahman explained his intentions to his friend, "I'm not trying to get to know him because of his black eyes. Rather I'm doing it for her eyes. I want to know him for a specific purpose. My aim is the waitress, not some beggar whose head looks like a cognac bottle. This isn't a clochard's friendship." He spoke those words and bent his head over his chest.

26

They left the bar totally drunk and were met at the door by a Filipino prostitute. When the philosopher smiled at her, she turned to him and opened her coat, revealing a short skirt, dark thighs, and provocative breasts. He asked if she would accompany him to his apartment, and she said yes. She walked with the two men until Ahmad went off on his own. The two friends agreed to meet the following day at noon.

27

Abd al-Rahman and the prostitute returned to his apartment under a heavy rain that was soaking into Paris. The rain didn't stop all night, and the streets filled with puddles that shone like pieces of glass under cars' headlights. The philosopher was in the habit of going home drunk every night after spending hours in bars drinking and talking, eventually leaving with a different prostitute each night. This was his way of fighting his loneliness and isolation. His anger at others and his swearing were not deliberate insults but an expression of noble desperation. He was suffering, and in his condition his only consolation was his belief that philosophy can be attained only through suffering, pain, and tragedy.

The afternoons passed quickly during the Parisian winters but the nights were like a wet and icy nightmare. To overcome his anguish Abd al-Rahman had nowhere to go but the bars and bordellos. Every now and then he spent time quarreling with his friend Ahmad, an Iraqi who had come to Paris to study engineering but never got a degree. He survived in the French capital through the largesse of rich Iraqis, for whom he did small favors in exchange for cigarettes, a drink, or a sandwich. He would always return drunk to his hotel room in Porte d'Italie, enter his cold room, lie down on his bed, cover himself with a damp blanket, and drop off to sleep.

28

The following morning the sun made its appearance between the clouds, warming up a wet Paris day that was still filled with the previous night's rain. Ahmad pushed at the door of Apartment 13 in one of Gay-Lussac's buildings just as the Filipino prostitute was rushing out without makeup and carrying her evening clothes. He gave his friend, who was still in bed, the morning papers: *Le Monde*, *Le Figaro*, and *Libération*. This ritual was followed by breakfast, which Ahmad habitually prepared for the two of them.

After skimming the papers, the philosopher took a shower and prepared himself for the activities of the new day. He wanted to know what plans had been laid for meeting Si Muammar, a scheme that would protect his pride and dignity as a philosopher. Ahmad pressed for an informal encounter, explaining that the matter was not worth formalities. He spent a great deal of time with the Algerians and knew them well, so he advised Abd al-Rahman simply to ask Si Muammar about conditions in Algeria as an overture to their conversation. The philosopher objected, clearly unhappy with Ahmad's suggestion. He insisted on meeting him in a "philosophical manner."

"I've learned that he has an Algerian girlfriend and an Iraqi friend named Nader," explained Ahmad.

"He's a crook then—an Algerian girlfriend. He's a crook," commented Abd al-Rahman, laughing victoriously and clapping. He continued, "Despite all this I want to meet him in a special way. I want to humiliate him, to crush him from the first moment. You want me to go and tell him that I wish to become acquainted with him? Impossible!"

He fell into a reflective mood, trying to think. In truth, the philosopher was unable to think during crucial moments; instead he dreamed in his own philosophical way. He wondered aloud why his friend wasn't thinking like he was, in a philosophical manner. Surprised, Ahmad was quick to explain, "Because you're the philosopher, not me."

Abd al-Rahman was trying to think of a dignified way to meet his rival, an arrangement worthy of his social and philosophical rank. He didn't want to stoop to the level of the common people and the pseudo-philosophers to reach his aim. After some deliberation he came up with an approach that Ahmad had suggested previously but which he had rejected. He presented the same idea in a slightly different way so as not to appear to contradict himself: "We can go to the Latin Quarter and have you ask the Iraqi philosopher to discuss some of Sartre's ideas with Si Muammar."

Ahmad expressed his huge admiration for the suggestion. He knew the philosopher could not stand to have anyone contradict him, even in simple matters, like many young people of his generation. As far as Abd al-Rahman was concerned, disagreeing with him meant failing to recognize his genius. This would lead the philosopher to cross that friend off his list, insult him, and even resort to physical assault. Ahmad, however, could not afford to lose the friendship and approval of a supporter. He was neither a philosopher nor a politician and barely a human being. All he wanted was to stay alive, even if it meant surviving, like cats and dogs, on the master's scraps. He was willing to go along with Abd al-Rahman's mistakes, accept them without argument, and humbly accept blame for the philosopher's failures, and beg for forgiveness.

The two men left the Gay-Lussac apartment around noon in search of Si Muammar. The philosopher now considered Muammar a disturbed man and a drug addict, who was loose, adventurous, lustful, and destructive. Making his way through the crowds, Abd al-Rahman felt distant and alone, a sentiment that provided him with a sense of strength. He walked firmly and forcefully, his face pale and his nose red from the cold. A light wind teased women's hair as they walked laughing, carrying their books. He overheard snatches of love stories, philosophical discussions, and political debates as he moved between the patrons of sidewalk cafés and restaurants. He heard music noticed the window displays of bookstores, and saw the huge selection of flowers arrayed in beautiful containers. They passed cigarette and newspaper kiosks, telephone booths, and souvenir shops along the way.

Abd al-Rahman followed behind Ahmad, who was searching for Si Muammar in the cafés along their route until they found him sitting with some of his Algerian friends and Nader, the Iraqi. Relieved, he pointed him out to Abd al-Rahman. Si Muammar's profile looked like that of a typical Algerian—thin, pug-nosed, with a skillfully shaped mustache over a delicate mouth. He had curly hair with some graying and was balding slightly.

The two friends sat at a nearby table. As soon as the philosopher looked closely at Si Muammar he panicked. His heart began pounding and his hands trembled, his eyes turned red and teary and he started panting. He whispered to Ahmad, "What are we doing here?" Nonplussed, Ahmad didn't know what to say and looked at the philosopher with his mouth agape. When he heard him say, "Let's go," Ahmad objected, "After coming all this way?!" The philosopher grew confused and fearful, but agreed to stay in order "to rest a little."

The situation revealed Abd al-Rahman's weak character, but why would a philosopher need a strong personality? It's his mental acuity, strong philosophical background, and vision that count. A personality is shaped by external factors and social and economic conditions. Philosophy needs an inner hunch, a certain premonition about the destruction of the external world that causes the philosopher to shun the outside world, despise it, and ignore it. Abd al-Rahman's personality was shaped from the inside, and from this inner structure came the strength of his ideas and concepts, but it also made him more fearful of others. His introverted nature hindered his interaction with women, yet he was grateful for a weakness that protected him from acting foolishly, like the homeless sleeping in metro stations, the drunkards in the bars, and the beggars on the sidewalks who were adventurous and paid the price for it. Sudden bouts of courage often placed him in ridiculous situations that he greatly regretted.

Ahmad was surprised to hear him declare, "Who is this clochard who intimidates me?!" Ahmad agreed with him, somewhat concerned by his reaction, and asked whether he should go talk to Si Muammar. Abd al-Rahman asked him to wait a little. While Ahmad was waiting for an answer, the philosopher pretended to be reading a newspaper to give himself time to regain his courage and come to a decision. Abd al-Rahman instructed Ahmad, "Go to him and tell him that the Iraqi existential philosopher wants to discuss with him topics related to existentialism in Algeria." Ahmad rushed over to Si Muammar's table, approached the man, and whispered a few words in his ear, causing both Si Muammar and Nader to burst out laughing. Abd al-Rahman watched closely, his heart racing.

Ahmad returned to his friend in a state of confusion, not knowing what to tell him, and at a loss as to what should be their next step. "Let's run."

"What?!" asked a surprised Abd al-Rahman.

"I am telling you, let's get out of here." The philosopher didn't understand.

"Why? What did he tell you?"

Ahmad explained, "He made fun of me. He told me, 'let him go to Sartre and discuss the subject with him.'"

Ahmad was shaking and ready to bolt. Abd al-Rahman was deeply humiliated and saddened, not only because this Algerian clochard had made fun of him and insulted him, but also because he had missed an opportunity to fulfill his aim. This turn of events meant that he would never be able to reach the waitress of Café de Flore. He was furious because Ahmad had failed to find the right words in French to accomplish his mission; he probably hadn't expressed himself properly. Though innocent of all those accusations, Ahmad accepted responsibility for his failure, "Yes, it's my fault. Please forgive me."

While Ahmad was absorbed in his mea culpa, Si Muammar and Nader approached the philosopher and asked if both men were Iraqis. Ahmad confirmed their origins. Abd al-Rahman remained very calm as Nader and his friend sat down at their table. Abd al-Rahman eyed Si Muammar rather anxiously, and to break the ice Si Muammar asked him how long he had been in Paris.

"I arrived three years ago," said Abd al-Rahman.

The philosopher did not feel like engaging in a philosophical discussion with Si Muammar while Nader was present. He wanted to do that another day in the presence of the waitress, in order to impress her and to show Si Muammar what it meant to be a philosopher. He engaged in casual conversation, reluctant to reveal his true intentions. Nader, a simple, goodhearted young man, soon turned the conversation to the direction of philosophy, asking Abd al-Rahman whether he was an existentialist.

"Yes, I am an existentialist. What about you two?"

Nader said no, and Si Muammar said, smiling, "This depends on one's understanding of existentialism." He then lit a cigarette without offering any to the others. Abd al-Rahman quickly took his pack of cigarettes from his coat pocket and offered one to Nader, who declined, explaining that he was not a smoker.

Si Muammar turned to Abd al-Rahman and asked, "What does existentialism mean to you?"

Abd al-Rahman's answer was ready, in French, one that he had memorized from one of the most famous philosophy encyclopedias of his time. Without hesitation or embarrassment he launched into a comprehensive and complete definition of existentialism. He sat back, eyes half closed, moistened his lips with his long red tongue, took a deep breath, and said, "Existentialism is a tendency hostile to the absolute outlook that represses cases of differences and absence of continuity in practical life. This enmity," he took a deep puff from his cigarette, "takes the form of profound self-analysis and calls for the priority of existence over essence. Therefore, it takes a biased position in favor of the partial," he took a light puff, "and the material against any effort meant to reach a complete doctrine under which all actions can be classified. This is where the existential philosopher finds sympathy for a doctrine that confirms the superiority of the active mind over the theoretical mind."

He hardly had time to catch his breath after delivering this amazing definition of existentialism than Si Muammar and Nader burst out laughing noisily. They cried laughing, and Nader couldn't contain himself. Ahmad and Abd al-Rahman were silent in their total disbelief of the reaction of the two men. They could not understand why these two stupid men would laugh at a definition available in the greatest and most expensive encyclopedia of philosophy in France, *Larousse Encyclopedia.*

Si Muammar explained apologetically that he wasn't very familiar with philosophy. "Pardon me, my friend. I don't understand this philosophy stuff at all. I'm a down-to-earth fellow, fun-loving and pleasure-seeking. I like drugs, I'm lazy—this is my philosophy."

Upon hearing his explanation Abd al-Rahman and Ahmad burst out laughing, perhaps a little artificially. Abd al-Rahman said, "Excuse me, Si Muammar, but do you call those insignificant inclinations a philosophy? Those are things anyone can do. Even Ahmad, who understands nothing, can do them."

Si Muammar said in his own defense, "Why not? It's a philosophy that depends on the art of living an idle life."

Indignant, Abd al-Rahman asked, "Do you consider laziness a philosophy!"

Si Muammar went on explaining his way of life. "It's true; I don't work and I live off my girlfriend. I'm a parasite who feeds on other people's blood; this is my philosophy in life."

Ahmad asked him, "Are you proud of yourself?"

Before he could answer, Abd al-Rahman intervened. "Ahmad lives at my expense but he doesn't boast about it." He had no qualms about embarrassing his friend.

Si Muammar was amused and replied, "Why not? I am proud of it. Take colonialism for example. It feeds on the blood of the people that are colonized. I rejected it. I didn't put myself at its disposal. I don't contribute to life at all. I came to France to live off the colonizer's female population, and I'm totally at peace with myself. Their men sleep with our women there, and we sleep with their women here." Nader was greatly amused by Si Muammar's words.

Abd al-Rahman asked Si Muammar if he was studying philosophy at a Parisian university. "No," he replied. "I studied literature but I didn't finish my studies. I discovered that it all was a terrible lie, so I stopped. Those are all falsified facts, believe me." Abd al-Rahman asked him to explain what he meant, and Si Muammar happily obliged. "Literature and philosophy," he said, "are falsified facts established by the powerful and the wealthy, and I don't care for either literature or philosophy."

"What interests you then?" asked Abd al-Rahman.

"The sorcerers and the exiled." Nader interrupted. "Those are the wise men sleeping in the brothels in a fog of hashish." He then laughed loudly and was joined by Ahmad. Pressing his position, Abd al-Rahman asked, "Do you consider such matters a philosophy?"

Nader explained, "It's passive resistance." Abd al-Rahman asked him where he lived and evoked a lengthy explanation: "I live close to the Debussy Market. I have a room that overlooks the market, and I sleep to the sound of merchants, greengrocers, and the shouts of the grilled-chicken sellers. I like this place because it reminds me of the popular souks in the Arab world."

Soon after, their female Algerian friend arrived and greeted them with a hoarse *bonjour* in what sounded like the voice of a man coming out of the hammam. Si Muammar introduced her as his friend Aisha, calling his new acquaintances "our philosopher friends from Iraq," a designation that Abd al-Rahman disliked and considered a mockery. When they left, Abd al-Rahman and Ahmad sat face to face. The philosopher was clearly dismayed by the insignificant issues "that clochard" considered to be a philosophy.

The singular impression Si Muammar left on the philosopher was that he was a superficial man. Though Abd al-Rahman was well aware that philosophy was theoretical and that existentialism had a practical side, he also knew that the theory was its creative and foundational element. Everyone knows that existentialism came about as a reaction to abstract philosophy, but one must admit that abstraction is the basis of philosophy. Existentialism cannot reject abstraction without the aid of abstraction, since it is based on abstraction. Can, therefore, Abd al-Rahman be considered bereft of any philosophy?! If so, what would be the meaning of those superficial actions, totally lacking a theoretical framework or formulation, undertaken by pickpockets, beggars, thieves, and drug addicts?

Braking his silence, the philosopher declared, "This hashish addict seems proud of his ideas."

"He's superficial," said Ahmad.

Abd al-Rahman added, "Insignificant."

The truth of the matter is that Abd al-Rahman was interested in Si Muammar's words only to the degree they would help him reach the waitress. He felt this scoundrel did not need the waitress, because he had an Algerian girlfriend who physically was not bad at all, though her face was pale and skinny. Si Muammar seemed proud of their friendship and showed clearly that his relationship with the Café de Flore waitress was based only on casual interest, the parasitic relationship of a blood-sucking bug. Despite Si Muammar's political interpretation, his position was weak, simply the relation of an oppressed masculinity with a female symbolizing the conqueror. Making love to her was his way of taking his revenge and humiliating the colonizer.

Abd al-Rahman concluded that Si Muammar would give up his French girlfriend in the end, and he, Abd al-Rahman would win her over without any feelings of guilt. When he returned to his room in Gay-Lussac he realized that the encounter had not been a total success, but still the path to his waitress was now more easily traversed.

The event was magnified in his dreams and took on a heroic aspect. Head on the pillow, the philosopher saw a forest, streets, long alleys, two lakes separated by parks, and playgrounds. He imagined a horse-drawn carriage moving through the forest paths while the heavyset driver chatted about the importance of the place. Throughout the forest there were buildings, swimming pools, huge trees, and beautiful lakes. He saw himself walking with the waitress, lying on the ground with her, and relaxing in the shadow of a tree as he brushed over the panty-line beneath her skirt. A violin player added to the romantic atmosphere. Her lips were trembling and her eyes softening. She pulled him close and, shivering with pleasure, gave him a passionate kiss. Just then a bird let go its droppings into his eye. Unperturbed, he wiped them off, unwilling to stop kissing the waitress. The bird droppings continued to land on his face, however, and finally awakened him from his sleep. The upstairs tenant's bathroom had flooded and was leaking from his ceiling and onto his face.

29

Abd al-Rahman left his apartment and wandered along the Rue Saint-Michel. He was filled with a sense of energy, having awakened without the help of the alarm clock. He wanted to forget past events but was reluctant to give up thinking about the waitress, despite her unpleasant attitude toward him. He was convinced that she was nicer to Si Muammar, Sartre, and the other philosophers who frequented the café. He was somehow convinced that this was her way of being reserved with him or possibly a clever strategy on her part, an instinctive woman's skill. He found excuses for her comportment, but they were not in his favor.

He took the metro toward Saint-Germain-des-Prés. The train car was crowded, and the rush of passengers grabbing at the empty seats upset him immensely. He swore at them as he settled into a seat, thinking of the days ahead when he would become the waitress' lover. Their daily encounters at the café and elsewhere would make Si Muammar jealous, maybe even Sartre as well. This notion comforted him and made him more tolerant of the passengers getting on and off at each stop.

He hesitantly pushed open the door of Café de Flore and saw Sartre sitting at a table with Simone de Beauvoir and three other friends. Sartre was talking in an ugly voice that sounded like the Khudayri family's rooster. The waitress stood behind a wooden bar near Sartre's table. He approached her with a smile and was certain that Si Muammar had told her about him. She was wearing a smile that might be construed as an expression of admiration. He felt liberated, now convinced that his assumptions were correct and that the waitress had fallen head over heels in love with him. He desired her even more, and when he turned to her he was nervous. Her red lips, rosy cheeks, blue eyes, and bulging breasts made him dizzy. He fell silent when she asked him in a neutral tone, still smiling, "Would you like to order something?" In a soft and low voice he said, "No, no." A strong dart of desire convulsed him.

"Very good, then, you'll have to leave," she replied. He was shocked and asked for an explanation.

"You can stay if you order something." He provided a reason for his presence that he hoped would open up new horizons for him, "I came to see Si Muammar."

"He hasn't come in today," the waitress said and walked away coquettishly in her tight cream skirt and hip-hugging blue angora sweater. He could see her panty-line and again felt that electric shock of desire. There was bitterness in his mouth and a pang in his heart. All the feelings of relaxation he had felt when he entered the café were gone. Sartre's ugly voice sounded even uglier.

He walked down the street watching the wet flowers, his eyes on the women rushing in their white raincoats, looking stern, and advancing like military guards. He took a deep breath, gnashed his teeth, and decided to walk like the Frenchmen did, with big fast steps. He entered the Café le Jour, sat at a table, ordered a Turkish coffee, lit a Gauloise cigarette, and began thinking about the events of the day. The coffee tasted terrible, nothing like his usual coffee at Café de Flore.

30

He walked fast, pondering recent events. He considered his effort to become acquainted with Si Muammar one of his latest failures, a simple matter of fact, like a rejection by someone we like. It was a simple truth, the common denominator that ties together all those who fall in love. It's a triangle with conscience at one point, vice at another, and sex at the third.

This was a narrow outlook, but Abd al-Rahman turned his anticipated relationship with the waitress into a relationship with himself, a way of correcting a commonly held misconception that vice can be erased and conscience ignored, but sex remains the foundation upon which everything rests. Sex is a neces-sity, just like food, philosophical faith and religion, and normal bodily functions. He was wondering how he could restart the broken dialogue, meet Si Muammar and go with him to Café de Flore. They would talk like fast friends, and Si Muammar would treat him as an old and important colleague. He would introduce him to the waitress, and then leave the details to Abd al-Rahman. Later, there would be a reaction that neither he nor the waitress would be able to control, a sexual attraction that would shake them both to the core. Sex would acquire a central and philosophical significance for a changing life, for an end to the fear of the other's body, of otherness. The encounter would take place on the bed, this being the only place where violence ends.

This encounter would put an end to his inclination to destroy the world, as all his violent tendencies would be channeled into this concept, or what the philosopher calls the 'situation,' the most dramatic of all situations. He even considered it to be the most serious, the most essential, and the most specific. According to him it was disconcerting to neglect it, and he regretted his inability to get over this short moment, stop the torture of this debate, and refrain from seeing himself as a failure—rejected and alone. Was his anxiety over the case of the Café de Flore waitress stronger than his angst over death, existence, and fate? This was a constant preoccupation, though weak and superficial at times, but it was at least clear.

31

Abd al-Rahman walked all the way to Place Edmond Rostand. He didn't feel like going back to his apartment. He had mixed feelings, neither happy nor sad. He felt like watching the technicolor films at the Odéon cinema, the ones he had liked so much in Baghdad. He walked by the metro station, traffic lights, and many wonderful sights before reaching the cinema. Once the film began and he heard the music and became involved in the sentimental plot, he relaxed and very gradually became totally at ease.

32

When he left the theater, the cold had subsided but a fog had enveloped everything. He walked slowly in the night, wrapped in his thick coat, and took in the surroundings illuminated by the city lights. He stopped at a hotdog stand, ordered a hotdog with mustard, and smiled at the seller, remarking to himself how existentialist the scene was. As she was preparing his sandwich he said, "You know, that piled up roll reminds me of the French Revolution, when the revolutionaries impaled the king's supporters."

As he was eating his sandwich he saw Ahmad on the other side of the street. He called him over, and the two men walked together. Abd al-Rahman asked if he had seen Si Muammar, and Ahmad explained that he had only run into Nader in the Latin Quarter. "Didn't he tell you anything about Si Muammar? Hasn't he seen him?" Ahmad explained that Nader had not seen him and was, in fact, looking for him. Abd al-Rahman suggested they go looking for him in Place des Vosges. Ahmad advised him to wait until the following day, so the two of them spent the rest of the evening in a bar instead. The place was very dark except for a few faint lights. They could hear the noisy laughter of the drinking customers, and they soon joined them, ordering a bottle of whiskey and two glasses and kept on drinking in silence. When they left the bar they were both completely inebriated.

33

Before noon the following day Ahmad rushed into Abd al-Rahman's room and woke him. Disoriented and still half asleep, he asked what was happening. Ahmad shouted, "I saw Nader in the Latin Quarter and he gave me a piece of sad news."

Abd al-Rahman asked anxiously, "Something related to the Café de Flore waitress?"

"No, it's about Si Muammar. His brother was killed in Algeria fighting the occupation forces. He's a martyr."

"Will Si Muammar be leaving France then?" Abd al-Rahman asked calmly.

"Yes," said Ahmad.

Reflecting on the situation, the philosopher pondered, "He will have to fight against the colonialist now, won't he!"

Deep down Abd al-Rahman was elated by the news, yet he managed to hide his feelings by expressing an exaggerated concern about two issues, Algeria's future and existentialism. The Algerian revolution was growing, existentialism was leaning more and more toward revolution, and Abd al-Rahman was getting closer to his waitress. With Si Muammar's departure she would be left without a lover, and he would step in to replace him. She's French and wouldn't be able to last long without a lover.

Ahmad told Abd al-Rahman that Si Muammar had asked to see them, together with all his friends, to receive their condolences. Abd al-Rahman was elated. For the first time he felt that luck was on his side, as he was finally on his way to win the waitress. He'd have the opportunity to meet her through her friend, all obstacles would disappear, and he would be left alone with her after Si Muammar's departure. Once they started talking, she would get to know him and become attached to him like a Christian clings to his faith.

"This is great, great! This is my chance and I'll grab it," he said to a disgusted Ahmad, who didn't say a word but went into the kitchen to fix breakfast.

34

On Wednesday evening Ahmad and Abd al-Rahman arrived at the Café de Flore. It was raining heavily, and when they went in their coats were soaked. Si Muammar was standing at the bar, his face flushed and his eyes filled with tears. He was totally drunk and could hardly stand up straight. The waitress was trying to help him, but he pushed her away. Nader came to the rescue, held him by the shoulders, and tried to calm him down. The café was empty except for two young Frenchwomen and a blond young man who was observing the situation with great interest and emotion. The philosopher didn't know it, but he was witnessing the greatest struggle of the twentieth century and the end of western colonial power. He asked Ahmad what was happening, but Ahmad wasn't sure, though he found the scene awkward. Then they heard Si Muammar shout drunkenly, "Leave me alone."

In a strident voice the young Frenchman shouted, "Let him be. If he can't destroy the west he can at least tear down its culture."

"Leave me alone," repeated Si Muammar, staggering in the direction of a table piled with books. He swept them onto the floor, went to the bar, took a half-filled bottle of cognac, poured it over the books, and lit them with his lighter, laughing loudly. "Hey, brothers, clap now! The comedy is over." His tirade continued. "These are all imposters. Jean-Jacques Rousseau is a liar. Saint Simon is a liar with all his utopias. Voltaire is a lie, and so are Molière and Bergson. They deceived us, they deceived us. The biggest of all imposters is Sartre. He's a liar— a colonialist lie!"

The books burned quickly, making a cracking sound. The waitress stood behind Si Muammar looking forlorn as he named each author whose book he tossed onto the pile—Alfred de Musset, Montaigne. The flames reflected off the ceiling and walls of the café and onto Abd al-Rahman's face. He looked like a red ghost. Sartre's book *La nausée* did not burn with the other books. Nader pushed it closer to the fire with his foot. When the philosopher saw Nader's gesture he considered it a personal attack. He rushed to seize the book and save it from the fire and burned his hand in the process. He shouted, "Burn anything you want except this book. Burn anyone but Sartre." He emitted a stream of invectives at Si Muammar, Nader, and all the café customers. He rushed at Si Muammar and tried to strike him, but he had already slipped to the floor, too drunk to maintain his balance.

Having rescued *La nausée* from total destruction, the two friends left the bar quickly and with agitation. In their rush to leave they forgot their coats on that rainy and extremely cold Parisian night.

35

Si Muammar returned to Algeria, but the philosopher's joy at the news, which Ahmad reported to him, did not last. He soon learned that the waitress had left to join her lover there. This marked the end of a phase in the philosopher's life.

36

Abd al-Rahman's love for the Café de Flore waitress was a formative experience. He faced the definitive news of her departure for Algeria stoically, like the true and authentic existentialist he was in soul and mind. His was not an acquired existentialism like that of his contemporaries, the Arab poets, the philosophers, and the litterateurs who had been influenced by Suhail Idris or the existentialism transmitted by Abd al-Rahman Badawi in the journal *al-Katib al-'arabi*.

Though there were widespread rumors and gossip that questioned the philosopher's integrity, depth of experience, or the authenticity of his genius, his changing and unstable life provided proof of the opposite. It is important when scrutinizing his life to go all the way back to his childhood. It would be impossible to write the philosopher's biography without scrutinizing that stage of his life in order to establish the strong and glorious aspects of his thinking, a gargantuan philosophy that influenced a whole generation. His philosophy was shaped by his childhood experiences. He was an existentialist even then, and his nausea began when he spied on his parents in their bedroom, contrary to rumors that attribute it to Suhail Idris's novel *al-Hayy al-latini* (The Latin Quarter) published in 1953 in Beirut when that city was the capital of Arab culture. In reality the Iraqi existential philosopher was not influenced by this first existential Arabic novel, or *al-Katib al-'arabi*. There is no proof that he was influenced by the writings of Abd Allah Abd al-Dayim or Shaker Mustafa, or even the translated works of Emile Shuwairi. Those who believed that the *al-Adab* journal shaped his existential vision were wrong. Equally mistaken were those who claimed that he was influenced by a visiting Iraqi professor from Paris who gave a lecture on existentialism at the College of Humanities in 1951.

The truth is that despite its existential theme, Suhail Idris's novel in no way matches the nihilistic and profane life of the philosopher of al-Sadriya in the sixties. The writings of Abd Allah Abd al-Dayim and René Habashi published in *al-Adab* journal in the early fifties lacked a deep existential vision that could refute the philosopher's vision or even equal it. This is true of Professor Albert Nasri Nader's lecture at the College of Humanities and Emile Shuwairi's translations. In any case, the philosopher had strong reservations about those translations and doubted the correctness of Shuwairy's interpretation of the original text. What could those two scholars add for someone who was able to read Sartre in the original language?!

By pure coincidence, in a Paris bookstore Abd al-Rahman had found a biography of Sartre the same year he left Baghdad to study for his doctorate. That book was full of photographs of Sartre, members of his immediate and extended families, and some of his friends, and also included a number of childhood photographs. It was in this photograph album that the Iraqi philosopher discovered the close resemblance between himself and the French philosopher: the hairstyle that Sartre never changed and the facial features, except for his glasses and crossed eyes.

While he managed to duplicate the black plastic eyeglass frames with thick lenses, he had no way of simulating the crossed eyes. That failure remained a source of aggravation for the philosopher that lasted his whole life. Strangely enough, Sartre's father looked like Shawkat Amin, Abd al-Rahman's father, except for the headgear, the stick, and the coat. The philosopher's mother, Munira al-Hafez, resembled Sartre's mother as well, and even the philosopher's maternal uncle could have passed as Sartre's uncle's twin brother.

These discoveries moved the philosopher deeply. Back in his Paris apartment he was overcome by vertigo and fell out of his chair. He suddenly knew that he was destined to be a philosopher and realized that he belonged to a family of philosophers. As such, he was made for thinking, not working, and it fell to him to take those ideas back to his homeland.

His epiphany led him to surrender completely to the precepts of existential philosophy and to vow total allegiance to the philosopher's life. These feelings were compatible with his conceptions of his childhood and adolescence, in which he saw his parents as two great and mighty gods — handsome, heroic, pure, and wealthy — who looked after him and shielded him from his weaknesses and narcissism and saw to it that he grew up strong and able to confront the external threats of society. But as soon as their vigilance weakened, he became aware that his parents were not all he had imagined them to be and that there were other gods more beautiful, more powerful, and wealthier. It was as if he had fallen from the heights and discovered that familial love was a huge deception. At this early stage of confusion he only found solace in his thoughts or, worse, emptiness. His reaction was to invent a legend in which he was a child rescued and adopted by an unknown family nobler and purer than the parents who raised him. He held the woman who tucked him into bed in the cold winter nights to be his adopted mother; likewise with the man who acted as his father. He thought of himself as an illegitimate child.

This make believe opened up a dream world filled with strange stories that inclined him toward greater secrecy about his private life. He turned into an unmanageable child who got his way by shouting and lying. He became insatiable in every enterprise he undertook and in the sensual pleasures he sought. The changes all took place after he discovered the true nature of his parents' relationship when spying on them through their bedroom as they made love. It was mainly his father's role in his life that remained problematic for him and which had led to bouts of nausea since childhood. Thus, existentialism for the philosopher was not the result of formal education but rather had been deeply ingrained in him from his very beginnings—it was a pure existentialism, realized in the minute details of his private life.

37

Abd al-Rahman hated his mother mercilessly. His hatred was evident in his passion for the forbidden and his propensity for violence and rage. His mother had been a model of gentleness, and she was closest to his heart, almost a miraculous creature in his eyes. But her quiet, affectionate nature was stripped away by her son's violence and his inclination to hurt himself and thus torture her. He wanted to face her as a suffering child. In his dreams his mother would torture him to get him to confess that he had been spying on her in her bedroom. She would cut off his head, shave it bald, and cast it away from atop a cliff.

His indiscretion was unknown except to the few servants who pulled him out of the mud into which he had fallen after leaving the house one rainy night. His hatred for his mother and father festered from that day on. He didn't want to feel that he was the

offspring of a sinful union, thickly encrusted in blood, because
it is foul and disgusting. In his eyes, his mother and father lying
in bed together was tantamount to true adultery. Whenever he
traveled with his father by carriage through the Jewish quarter of
Baghdad he would be overpowered by the feeling that his father
had brought him there in order to throw him to the bloodsuck-
ers in this dirty ghetto, where thousands of Jews lived in narrow,
winding streets. The putrid smell of decay, blood, and offal rose
from the ditches. The odor was just like that of their lovemaking,
the same smell he had noticed through the door, opened just a
crack, to his parents' bedroom.

38

It all happened on a cold rainy evening when his mother carried
him to his bed, covered him with sheets and blankets, and told
him the story of the lizards that roam the halls of the house at
night. She was trying to lull him to sleep, promising to give him
things he liked, but he soon realized that his mother was preoc-
cupied by other matters and was in a hurry to bid him goodnight.
He saw a twinkle in her eye and a twitch in her face as she fibbed
to him. He pretended to fall asleep, and as soon as his mother
was reassured, she rushed to her room. He got out of bed and
went to his parents' bedroom.

When he peered into their room he saw his mother's naked
body move on the bed and his father squeezing her breasts in
his hands. They were feverishly engaged in lovemaking, and
the sight was nauseating to him. He couldn't believe what he
was seeing. As she moaned with pleasure, his mother's voice
sounded repugnant to him. He covered his ears.

He rushed down the stairs, threw open the main door, and
ran into the garden shouting hysterically. He was haunted by
the image of his mother, her face drained of innocence. She was

fading away like a squeezed pimple. She was a devil chasing him. He slipped and fell and lay in the mud, where the servants later found him and carried him home on their shoulders, water and mud dripping from his clothes.

In the morning all three ate breakfast together, but his mother avoided his eyes and did not talk to him, in an effort to ignore the events of the previous night. When his father went to parliament, his mother stayed in the living room to enjoy the morning sun, but Abd al-Rahman ignored her and avoided talking to her. The tension lasted a whole week.

The boy was withering away, and his nausea persisted, especially when he remembered the horrible sight he had witnessed that night. His mother, Munira al-Hafez, would go down to the living room where he was sitting on the couch near the window staring at the thick trees in the garden. As soon as she got close to him, with her blond hair pulled up, fair skin, pure white face, beautiful neck, and colored winter clothes, he would rush away to his room.

At the end of that week she could no longer bear being shunned by her son. She went to his room, hesitant at first, and switched on the light. He didn't move and kept his head buried in the pillow. Then he peeked at her furtively, his beautiful black eyes full of tears. He asked her in a hoarse voice, "What do you want?" then quickly hid his face in the pillow and cried loudly.

Standing at his bed, she replied, "I want to know what's wrong with you?"

He told her, "You know."

"I want to hear it from you," she insisted.

She sat on the bed and toyed with her diamond ring, her head bent. He turned to her, "You do know, don't lie."

She repeated, "I am not lying, but I want to hear it from you."

He shouted his reply, hardly able to breathe, "Hear what? Do you want me to tell you what you were doing with him?"

Munira al-Hafez was unable to persuade him. She was embarrassed by his demeanor but kept on trying to talk with him. She finally said, "When you grow up you'll understand," but he interrupted her, blurting out without looking at her, "I am old enough, old enough!"

"My son . . . ," she said, but she was overcome by a crying fit and couldn't finish her sentence. He hastened to repudiate their relationship, "I'm not your son. I'm not your son."

"How can you say that? You are my son. You are old enough to differentiate between a husband and a stranger. He is my husband and your father," she said. The boy was still in denial.

"He's not my father, I don't know him."

Still his mother insisted, "You don't have the right to say that. He is your father." Abd al-Rahman kept on denying his connection to his parents until a strong crying fit interrupted him and he hid his face with the feather pillows.

This exchange between mother and son went on for a long time, with the boy denying the paternity of his parents and asking to be returned to his biological parents. "You're not my parents, you're criminals, you took me away from my real parents and you must return me to them."

Nothing Munira al-Hafez said could convince him or stanch his anger, yet she kept at it, "It is natural, accepted by religion and life in general. Ask around you—the servants, anyone. It's normal."

Still he remained hostile, "Don't lie. The servants will talk about you the way they talk about Rujina."

The mother felt defeated and said to him, "Do you compare me to Rujina?"

"You are the same," he said, "I don't want to stay here. I want to leave. What do you want from me?"

His mother was furious. She asked, "Even if we were not your parents, how do you think you were brought into this world?"

He replied, "Through some other means, different from this shameful way."

Finally, sadly, she was convinced that there was no talking to him. She left his room and went downstairs completely shattered. Overwhelmed, she soon broke down sobbing. When her husband returned from work and saw her in that state, he was very angry and immediately went to his son's room. He tried to talk to him, but in vain. He tried to convince him but failed. The boy did not utter a word in his father's presence.

39

The philosopher's life thereafter was in some ways a reaction to what he considered his mother's false purity. He was compelled to seek out all of the basest feelings and most sordid practices. In the Jewish quarter, a rather intimidating place for him, he found many things that fed his passions and inflamed his imagination and emotions. He went there with the servants—the groom, the carriage driver, and the gardener. It was a kind of purgative, a certain attachment to wild, tainted beauty. He saw beauty in the cats on garbage dumps and stray dogs covered with mud on rainy days. He liked watching the rats come out of the gutters and the donkeys driven by ruffians, and he found it all very attractive. He sought those sights during his evening walks in his grandfather's opulent gardens that stretched to the surrounding villages. He was searching for a balance in his life and a way that would teach him how to weigh matters and judge others.

The pure woman in Abd al-Rahman's life was replaced by dissolute women, the innocent woman by experienced women. He abandoned his imagination to obscene feminine traits, making scullery maids the major players in his life. He shared his mother's disgust for his father's addiction to alcohol, but he was disgusted with both of them for their bedroom relationship. He found the drunkenness of the carters and the obscene relationship between the carriage driver Saadun and the housemaid Rujina purer, deeper, and stronger than that of his parents. In his eyes Rujina was the ideal feminine person, despite her sluttish behavior. He became attached to her; she represented sin by excellence. All the others—the teamsters, drivers, thieves, servants, watchmen, and especially the gutter cleaners—he felt were the greatest beings to have emerged from the dregs of the earth. He contrasted his parents' clean clothes and elegance with the filthiness of the workers and concluded that their squalor was due to idleness. He felt an odd sexual attraction to what he saw as their mysteries and oddities. He saw them as primitive animalistic creatures, nobler somehow than his sanitary family members.

40

Abd al-Rahman's mother had a quiet beauty. She was fair skinned, white as cotton, but she had now lost much of her attractiveness and looked sad because of her son and his odd behavior. She was desperate. She loved her husband and never thought of any other man. She would have lived as the sole mistress in this big house were it not for the presence of her mother-in-law, a haughty Turkish woman who shared her authority. She made great concessions in order to live with her kind husband who respected his parents and listened to their advice. He, too, loved his wife. Under the spell of her beauty, he liked to spend time in her company. She spent most of her days, especially the afternoons, in the living room near the sunny window, working on her embroidery.

As a child Abd al-Rahman used to walk behind his mother or sit facing her on his father's lap, admiring her clear eyes that were so full of energy and her beautiful clothes. Much of that disappeared after she became ill and her beauty faded.

41

Abd al-Rahman's relationship with his mother turned harsh, and
he responded rudely to her affection and entreaties. The sight
of the intimate life of his parents had warped the philosopher's
behavior, his individual weaknesses, and his passive-aggressive
inclinations. The result was frequent escapades, chaotic sexual
conduct, much pain, and a sustained attitude of revolt He was
haunted by nightmares that continued throughout his adolescence. He would see himself dismembered and left lying on
asphalt streets. His childhood was transformed into a valley of
tears, dissatisfaction, and crying every time his mother spoke to
him. He attacked his father with a kind of hysteria at the slightest sign of affection, and their relationship became very strained.
He had an innate inclination for existentialism and so gradually
turned into a drunk philosopher, a Don Juan who changed partners frequently, a hedonist who enjoyed life more than he would
have had he chosen the moral path, as had his peers among the
aristocratic families.

42

The first woman to awaken his sexual instincts was Rujina the
maid. She was cleaning the marble stairs one morning. He stood
in front of her and raised his arms for her to carry him. She
squeezed his head between her breasts, where he smelled her natural sexuality, then put him down and caught him gently between
her thighs. The experience left him dizzy. He sat down on a couch
in the living room and closed his eyes for a few minutes. When
he opened them he saw Rujina sweeping the floor, her dark, full
thighs purposely uncovered. He was overcome with a deep sexual desire that drove him upstairs to his room. When he reached
the door he took another look at the lower floor and saw Rujina's
dark, lustful eyes staring at him. The fullness of her breasts was

evident from her cleavage, and her dress was pulled up above the knees. She winked at him as he went into his room.

43

Rujina had come to the house after Abd al-Rahman's mother fired the previous maid. Saadun brought her, and it gradually emerged that he had a relationship with her. The philosopher's father learned of their relationship but didn't mind as long as it didn't interfere with their work.

Rujina came from a Christian village north of Mosul. It was a rather primitive place, but she was not lacking in taste and refinement. She transformed the house into an impeccably clean and attractive residence. When he learned of her relationship with Saadun, Abd al-Rahman became attached to her. He was attracted by sinful urges that he found fascinating. He wanted to spy on her while she was in the bathroom or in her bedroom. He wanted to savor that body that had stirred something in him the day he watched her as she was cleaning the stairs.

Her eyes disturbed him and made it impossible for him to look straight at her. He cared more for her than he did for his own mother. He wanted to forget the horrible sight he had spied in his parents' bedroom. He wanted to regain his state of grace without sin. He began establishing a comparison between his mother's lovemaking with his father, a sin in his eyes, and Rujina's sinful life. He became enamored of the evil spirit, the evil and sin, when he heard Rujina's seductive story about her adulterous relationship in Talkif, her village.

44

Rujina was the daughter of Yusif, the owner of a bar on the outskirts of the village. She had been in love with Yaqo since adolescence, and he used to take her to a distant walnut tree to mess around. She was completely seduced by this son of a thief, whose father had come to Talkif thirty years ago from the village of Inshki. He bought large plots of land between Talkif and Betnaya. When he was murdered, his only son, Yaqo, inherited all his property. The young man was handsome but cruel and heartless, and intent on exercising his control over all the inhabitants of Talkif. If any one of them became too powerful, Yaqo bought up his property and threw him out of the village.

45

One day Yaqo went to Yusif's bar and began drinking. He told the owner that he wanted to buy the bar, took out his purse, and placed it on the counter. Yusif refused to sell and asked Yaqo to leave. "Do you know who you're talking to?" asked Yaqo. Yusif responded, in front of everyone present, by spitting in Yaqo's face. Yaqo went after him with a bottle of arrack, but the waiters intervened. Yaqo threatened Yusif angrily, telling him, "I will rape your daughter and spit on your face."

Two days later Rujina ran away from home and went to Yaqo's house with the help of Saadun, who used to look after Yaqo's horses. She gave herself to the rich landowner, and Saadun broadcast the news of Yaqo and Rujina's marriage to the whole village the following Sunday. When Yusif heard the news, he closed his bar and went home. He collapsed on the front steps and died of consternation on his daughter's wedding day.

46

Two months after the wedding Yaqo lost interest in Rujina and began spending time with a mistress. He left Saadun in charge of his household and horses while he took to drinking and gambling.

Rujina became Saadun's mistress and received him openly in her bedroom. He had a good deal for sure: enjoying the land, money, and Rujina. It became known throughout the village that Rujina had a Muslim lover. Her cousin Michael was furious and tried to kill Saadun, but the shot only hit him in the shoulder. Fearing for his life, Saadun ran away, never to be seen again, while Michael stayed on Yaqo's property to protect Rujina.

One day Michael got drunk and saw Rujina half naked in her room; he tried to rape her, but she pushed him away and hit him over the head with an iron bar. Before he died, Michael confessed to the investigator that Rujina had acted in self-defense when he tried to rape her. Rujina was released from prison and left Talkif for good. She took the first train to Baghdad, where Saadun was waiting for her.

Saadun took Rujina to his employer's house, and the same evening he recommended her as the new maid. From that day forward Rujina worked as a housemaid for the respectable Amin Shawkat. There she stirred the passions of the young boy who was growing up before her eyes. She was aware of the limits of his sexuality, however, and increased the dosage gradually. From his encounters with her he concluded that this woman was greater than the pure woman and the tainted woman superior to the clean woman. The woman who prostituted herself was far greater than the white dove. Abd al-Rahman was more familiar with the physicality of tainted creatures, and they inspired his thinking.

47

One day, as Abd al-Rahman was going downstairs, he heard the sound of the servants' shower near the kitchen. He guessed that Rujina was taking a shower, and this motivated him to go to the door. His heart was racing. He was torn between desire and panic, and fearful of being caught he almost ran away. Curiosity prevailed. He peeped through the keyhole and saw Rujina under the shower, her naked body luxuriating under the hot water. He stared at her round breasts, her dark nipples, where he knew the pleasure was. The sight of her smooth thighs, slim legs, and delicate hips excited him, and he struggled to see more through the narrow keyhole. Suddenly he heard a noise close by, and when he turned his head he saw Saadun smiling at him. Embarrassed, he tried to justify his being there, "I was trying to find out who was in the bathroom."

"I want to know too," said Saadun, still smiling, then pushed the boy aside and looked through the keyhole. He knocked three times, and Rujina let him in and locked the door behind him. Abd al-Rahman wanted to run away and hide in his room, but when he heard the sound of the running water and the moans of pleasure coming from behind the door he peeped through the keyhole again and saw the two naked bodies touching gently under the hot water, surrounded by white steam.

48

He often recalled the exciting scene he had glimpsed through the keyhole. It was a fascinating image that remained forever embedded in his mind. Such vivid images fueled his imagination and were revived every time he showered.

49

Saadun, the carriage driver, was a very elegant man. His clothes were old and worn from frequent ironing, but they were clean. His thick hair had a few streaks of white, but his mustache was black. His piercing gaze and stern features made a strong impact. One day a relative of the family saw him leaving the garden in the direction of the stable, carrying a tray. She asked the lady of the house about him, "It's Saadun. He looks after our horses." The woman laughed loudly, "He has the face of a master and does the work of a servant."

50

After the bathroom incident the young boy became attached to Saadun. They often went on walks and outings together, and Abd al-Rahman liked Saadun's proud demeanor, his eloquence and his ability to seize an opportunity without hesitation. Those were qualities he himself lacked.

One day Abd al-Rahman was out walking in the garden when he saw Saadun washing his hands, preparing to go out. Saadun smiled at the boy, opened the main door, and left. The boy ran after him and asked him where he was going.

"Would you like to come along?" asked Saadun.

"Yes," replied the boy.

"Go tell your father that you're coming with me." Abd al-Rahman's father, wearing his traditional clothes, was observing the scene from the second floor balcony. Before the boy spoke the father nodded his head approvingly.

51

The two walked together through the muddy path that separated the house gardens from the surrounding fields. Saadun was whistling and walked fast, taking long steps, his hands in his pockets. The boy hurried behind, stopping every now and then to remove a pebble or a piece of fruit that had fallen from tree. When they reached the main road, they headed toward the city drainage stations, where many fellahin fleeing the harshness of their feudalistic masters had established a shantytown

They came to the city looking for work as unskilled laborers, shoeshine boys, cigarette vendors, hawkers, gardeners, or café servers. The Baghdadis called them al-Shuruqiya.

Saadun and Abd al-Rahman crossed the muddy wall that separated the shantytown from the street. Young boys swam in the dirty swamps with water buffalo fighting tick bites. The smell was unbearable, and the sight of putrid garbage was disgusting, but they soon left this squalid part of the city. They headed toward a group of mud houses behind the huts until they reached a small café with a broken wooden door. Chairs were lined up in front. As soon as they sat down, Ramadan the waiter rushed to offer them two cups of hot tea that they then enjoyed under a warm winter sun. Some other customers, who were playing dominoes, recognized Saadun's voice and came over. They hugged and greeted him, asking, "What brings you, Saadun? How are you?" Someone tossed two oranges to Saadun. Abd al-Rahman picked up the one that fell under the table and put it in his pocket. Said, the barber whose shop was near the café, came over and greeted Saadun.

"Oh, son of a bitch." Saadun laughed. "We're all children of bitches."

Said looked very much like Saadun. He slapped him on his belly, hugged him, and said to those present, "This is not my brother, this is the devil himself."

Saadun was soon surrounded by other acquaintances—Salman, Mahmoud al-Qantarji, who was reading the newspaper, and Jabbar. They were talking loudly, cracking jokes, and laughing. Meanwhile Abd al-Rahman was busy observing the street facing him. It was crowded with small carts, motorcycles, and wooden buses that were bursting with people. Cages holding hens and birds, and crates filled with milk containers were strapped on top. The buses were sloshing through the mud, each moving in a different direction, some toward

Tayaran Square, and others toward Bab al-Sheikh or Bab al-Sharqi. The boy enjoyed watching all the action but was too timid to ask questions.

Mahmoud invited Saadun and the boy to lunch, but Saadun declined and got up to leave. They cheerfully bade their friends goodbye and headed to a nearby slaughterhouse. The butchers were standing outside their shops, knives at their waists, aprons stained with blood. Sheep were eating meat scraps and pieces of offal. The potholes in the street were filled with dry blood. The boy liked this type of dirt because he considered it honest.

The big-bellied slaughterhouse owner sat outside smoking a water pipe, his bald head shining in the sun. Women were carrying milk jugs, their feet wrapped in white fabric meant to protect them from thorns and dirt. Saadun and Abd al-Rahman stood at the entrance of the slaughterhouse and were soon approached by a fair young woman with skin as white as milk. She pretended to have missed the bus and said to Saadun in a hoarse voice, "We miss you." She blushed as she talked, and her black eyes twinkled.

Saadun laughed back at her and touched her lightly with his foot, whispering, "Tomorrow."

A bus driver called out his destination, "Bab al-Sheikh, Bab al-Sheikh," and she rushed off. From the bus she bade them goodbye with a tender gesture.

"Who's she?" asked Abd al-Rahman.

"A friend," replied Saadun proudly, "isn't she more beautiful than Rujina?" The boy was quiet as they both walked back to the house.

52

Abd al-Rahman relived those images on their way back. He compared them to his family and the whole Iraqi bourgeoisie's extreme concern with appearances, hiding their dirt under starched collars and clean white shirts. Each day he discovered a different life with Saadun, the gardeners, the washers, the maids, and the driver.

The boy's dislike for his family and his relatives grew day by day. He was critical of their inability to enjoy life and have fun, to live in the fast lane, or enjoy physical contact. Those who were unable to perform popular heroic acts he judged harshly and determined a person's importance solely from appearance. He was resentful of their clothes and their mere existence, their strange illnesses, their annoying voices. He disliked women who did not look like Rujina, with her pure dark face, curly hair, mysterious eyes—and that crime of hers that so stirred his desires. He remembered how she had flirted with him without any feelings of embarrassment.

53

At first Abd al-Rahman was not able to establish contacts with people easily. He couldn't accept the fact that sex was a natural matter, as if he wanted to eternalize his childhood. He wanted to act in a responsible manner, like a mature individual, without tripping.

During his adolescence, as his masculinity was developing, he felt he was a sacred child. He didn't want to be like the adults and adopt their values, and he didn't consider the family sacred. Rather, he wanted to contest all that. Among those around him, Saadun relegated people to the past; Rujina had a past but no family, having even gone as far as to destroy her family; Suleiman the gardener worked to be able to live in the khan; and all Naser wanted was his bottle of arrack. On the opposite side were the large, complex families whose members, both men and women, were dragged down by a life of habits.

He mercilessly ridiculed the families in his parents' circle that he disliked so much, doing his best to assail their narcissistic feelings. He wanted to denounce them and thereby scare and shock his family.

One day he asked Saadun if he was married. Saadun laughed, "No. For what?"

Surprised, Abd al-Rahman wondered aloud, "Oh! What's the point in having a woman?"

"A married man has one woman, but a single man has many women." Saadun explained.

54

Abd al-Rahman belonged to an aristocratic family, although he did not experience the life enjoyed by his grandfather in his glorious heyday. He was a refined man who had been quite powerful during the Ottoman period. Abd al-Rahman grew up at a time when his family was losing its prestige, position, and power. He was not at all unhappy with his family's turn of fortune and enjoyed seeing it lose the standing and esteem it had once enjoyed. His grandfather did not talk much as he got older and began to wither away. His mustache, which he used to wear turned upward like a Turk's, now drooped. He could not help himself and needed to be carried like a child between the garden and the living room. His eyes wilted, and he covered his hair, which had by now turned gray, with an impeccably clean white Turkish cap. A woolen robe covered his combed-cotton pajamas and woolen slippers. He would plant his silver-clad cane and speak with his son in a low voice. He spent most winter days on the covered balcony, where he was protected from the wind and could enjoy the warmth of the sun. He drank his Turkish coffee there. When he wanted to sleep, the servants carried him to his room.

His grandfather was one of the most prominent figures in Baghdad during the time of Sirri al-Kraidi, who became Baghdad's wali in 1890. He established the park in Midan Square and, thanks to the astrologers, got close to Sultan Abd al-Majid and spent time at the palace admiring the beautiful gold-clad slaves and young boys from al-Karj. He often spoke of the meals that were served in the palace, the richly set tables, and the food served from gold and silver vessels. He described the cutlery, the pitchers, the glasses, and the incense burners. He married a Turkish woman named Nazla Hanim, and the couple went to Baghdad during the plague days. Right off she was shocked by the city's ugliness, unhealthy air, unattractive people, and bad food, and she immediately returned to Istanbul. Her husband later joined her, and this is when he met Wali Hasan Wafiq, who joined him in his walks around Istanbul. They were usually preceded by a detachment of horse riders, the slaves of the wali, and another regiment of foot soldiers in military dress, with English guns, and pipes and drums.

The family lost all this prestige during the royal era. Nazla Hanim said the king was good for nothing.

55

Abd al-Rahman spent his teenage years with Saadun wandering the parks, sitting at a café after school, working in the garden and the stable, and even playing poker in Khan Mamu at Bab al-Sheikh. Though his family knew about Saadun's exploits they didn't consider expelling him. Abd al-Rahman's mother caught him twice with Rujina, but she didn't make a fuss about it and satisfied herself with a reprimand. She explained clearly the reasons for her tolerance, "If it were not for my son's attachment to you, I would have expelled you long since." Her husband had once surprised them in a flagrant position in the kitchen as well.

56

Abd al-Rahman's father came upon them in the kitchen a little after midnight when he went down to investigate a suspicious noise. He threw open the door suddenly and turned on the light. The couple was lying on the floor totally naked. Shaken, Rujina stood in front of him without covering herself, while Saadun rushed to get into his clothes. Shawkat Amin's eyes dwelled on Rujina, who was in no hurry to cover herself. She collected her clothes and went to her room, moving provocatively. After she left, the father reprimanded Saadun, using the same words that his wife had chosen as the reason for keeping him.

The following day Abd al-Rahman awoke to news of the incident, but that night he saw his father sneak into Rujina's room. He told Saadun about his father and both found the story amusing. Saadun later offered to take the boy to a brothel, and they decided that they would go the following day.

57

The carriage moved slowly down the wet street where a light rain had fallen. Abd al-Rahman was sitting under the black top in the rear of the carriage, taking in the large illuminated posters on al-Rashid Street. He saw signs for Mackintosh English toffee, Van Heusen shoes, the Café Brazil, the Orosdi Back department store, and Jaqmaqji records. Under the reflections of movie house marquees, shop windows displayed gleaming luxuries. Abd al-Rahman was totally absorbed by the sights and wanted to hug the women coming out of the boutiques, posh cafés, and cinema houses.

On such outings Abd al-Rahman's liked to stop on al-Rashid Street at Dikket Bab al-Agha to smoke a water pipe, take in a film at the Roxy cinema, or even eat the kebab seller's semi-fresh food, sold near Mackenzie's bookshop. Dressed in his black suit necktie, and cap, he would sit on a metal chair and take in the liveliness of the market around him. Far from his father's hypocrisy and his mother's feminine purity and controlled coldness, he loved listening to the popular accent, the boastfulness of the people, the putrid odors. When Saadun asked if he wished to stop this time, he declined. "Don't stop today unless it's for a prostitute," he laughed loudly. They had hardly reached the end of al-Rashid Street, near the square facing the church, however, when he was overtaken by such fear and anxiety that his knees began knocking.

58

Saadun stopped the carriage at the entrance of the narrow alley overlooking al-Rashid Street from the far side of al-Harj market. The prostitutes who stood in front of the house were half naked and unashamedly exhibiting their charms and heavy makeup. Their coarse words evoked laughter. Abd al-Rahman and Saadun stepped out of the carriage and crossed the street toward the alley. The boy's legs were buckling under him. He was intimidated by the power of the prostitutes, and, self-conscious of his inexperience, he was unable to face them. One of them approached him and asked the boy to follow her. Her face, covered with heavy makeup, betrayed her age, her hair was dyed bright red, she smelled of alcohol, and she was scantily dressed. As soon as Abd al-Rahman heard her say, "Come with me," he ran away as fast as he could back to the carriage, breathing with great difficulty. He heard the prostitute laughing and calling after him, "Don't be scared! Come on, I won't bite you." He raised his head from his hiding place to check out the situation and saw Saadun talking with the woman. Both went inside the house.

Abd al-Rahman was perplexed by this sexual traffic. He saw respectable men enter the narrow alley in their posh cars.

Prostitutes wearing expensive clothes, jewelry, and fur coats, met and rode off with them. Toothless old women were doing the bargaining and collecting the money. Other young women were standing in the doorways; the male customers looked them over, and then took them into the house.

Twenty minutes later Saadun came out of the house, disheveled, closing his fly, his shirt half undone. He was laughing and shouted at the boy, "Don't worry, I won't bite you." When he reached the carriage he said to the horse, "Don't be upset. If there were prostitutes for horses I would take you to them."

Abd al-Rahman laughed at his apprehensiveness. The two men drove back to the fish restaurant near the church.

59

The restaurant was in a modest district of town, but the night and darkness hid the decrepit houses and the poverty of the place. The two men sat on a couch covered with woolen rugs, ready for their fish dinner; the smell of fried fish filled the place. Saadun lit two cigarettes and gave one to Abd al-Rahman. While they were waiting to be served, a woman in an abaya passed by coquettishly. Saadun's eyes followed her silhouette until she disappeared from view and he said, "She could break metal." The comment amused the boy, who was constantly amazed at Saadun's sexual prowess and unflagging interest in women. Saadun recalled how the boy had run away from the prostitute and hid in the carriage like a rat, to Abd al-Rahman's great amusement. He asked the boy what he thought of Rujina.

"I don't know" he answered.

"You'd like to try it with her, wouldn't you?" Saadun asked. Abd al-Rahman was silent. Simultaneously he felt a cold shiver run through his veins and a warm feeling in his skin. They arrived home late, drunk with joy.

60

Shortly after midnight the following night, Abd al-Rahman opened his bedroom door and saw Rujina standing in the dim light of the hall. She was wearing a revealing muslin dress. He approached her, breathing heavily, his eyes filled with desire. He kneeled and caressed her thighs; they then went into her room. He suggested they go to the roof, but she was afraid someone might surprise them. She took off her clothes, lay on the bed, and called Abd al-Rahman to join her. He averted his eyes from her nakedness, which reminded him of his mother's body moaning under his father's hairy legs. He sat down on the bed softly, and she took his head in her hands and placed it against her warm breasts. He passed his lips over them. Suddenly the door flew open and the light switched on. The two jumped in terror and heard his father shout, "Adulterous woman! First me, and now my son too!? And in the same bed!"

61

Naked, the boy ran to his room, hurtling up the stairs. He was mortified to pass his mother standing in front of her bedroom on his way. He quickly covered himself, rushed into his room, and slammed the door shut behind him. They were even now: he had seen her naked, and now she had seen him naked. Still he couldn't forget how she had stood motionless as he was running up the stairs naked before her.

The philosopher's childhood certainly provided sufficient material to make a serious existentialist out of him. A single document stated that the al-Sadriya philosopher was deeply influenced in both his philosophy and conduct by Edmond al-Qushli. It was the only document of those I found, either among those the lawyer Butrus Samhiri had shown me when I visited him in his office, those owned by Hanna Yusif which he gave me at our first meeting, or even the important papers that were held by Sadeq Zadeh. Edmond al-Qushli, the assiduous Christian, who worked first as a translator for an Indian company then as a teacher at Frank Aini School, lived with his grandmother Adileh in the district facing Mahallet Jadid Hasan Basha in Baghdad. In the fifties he was considered an existentialist, in the sixties a Trotskyite. When he was young, people referred to him as 'Edmond son of Adileh.'

One wonders why Abd al-Rahman became the preeminent existentialist philosopher in Baghdad while Edmond al-Qushli turned his back on existentialism completely—he even fought against it. It is possible that Abd al-Rahman was a victim of a Trotskyite plot organized by Edmond al-Qushli, with the help of the great bourgeois of the time, Faraj Khaddouri. But in offering this theory we would face another hurdle: How did a proletarian Trotskyite join with a comprador bourgeoisie against an existentialist of the sixties, a descendant of an aristocratic family that had been in gradual decline from Ottoman times, to the monarchy, and later under the republic?

62

It is well known that Edmond al-Qushli became acquainted with existentialism at the end of the forties reading the Egyptian journal *al-Katib al-'arabi* edited by Taha Hussein. This contradicts the rumors spread by Iraqi philosophers of Abd al-Rahman's generation who claimed that they carried existential thought into Iraq. But Edmond had read Abd al-Rahman Badawi's translations of Arnold's writings and some of Sartre's articles on the subject long before the sixties. In the fifties, specifically in 1953, he became very attached to Suhail Idris, the existentialist Arab thinker and friend of Sartre's. He brought existentialism to Iraq from Paris in his suitcase, as the Iraqi existentialists like to say.

Edmond fell in love with Aida Matraji, who was the Arab Simone de Beauvoir in the fifties and the sixties. He had two photographs hanging on his wall in his grandmother Adileh's house, one of Sartre and Simone de Beauvoir and, on the opposite wall, a photograph of Suhail and Aida together. He considered Aida more beautiful than Simone de Beauvoir and Suhail Idris more handsome than Sartre, because Sartre was short and Suhail was tall. And while Sartre saw matters with one eye, Suhail regarded them with two. He also confided to his existentialist friend Sarkun Saleh—who was introduced to existentialism around the end of the Second World War, in the Waqwaq café in Antar Square—that he loved Aida because she was honorable, whereas Simone de Beauvoir lived her life as many Frenchwomen did and had known hundreds of men before she slept with Sartre. This explained why, according to him, Arab existentialism is greater and more honorable than French existentialism.

Edmond al-Qushli might also have been influenced by the Baghdadi journal *al-Fikr*, published by an Iraqi painter with the help of his mother, Hajjeh Zakiya Abed. The journal closed down when she died. It was the same journal in which Naim Qattan published a news item copied from the French press about a conference Sartre had given in Paris. The place was so packed that the police had to intervene to get help for those who fainted in the crowd.

Naim Qattan was introduced to existentialism through readings in French. One of the important documents that Hanna Yusif gave me, however, stated that Edmond al-Qushli was too young in the forties to be interested in philosophy. But it's a fact that he was influenced by one of his friends who used to frequent the Waqwaq café (it might have been Sarkun Saleh himself) and became familiar with existentialism through the journal *al-Katib al-'arabi*, where he read Arnold's translated articles and those of Abd al-Rahman Badawi.

63

Edmond used to go to the Waqwaq café every day, sit on the wooden couch covered with mats, drink tea, and smoke. The café was always crowded and warm. He would sit close to the large glass windows overlooking the street to watch the passersby while listening to the sounds of classical music—Bartók, Debussy, Rubenstein.

Other café habitués were Husain Mardan, who always sat at a remote table in the corner. He would usually be joined by Boland al-Haydari and Fuad al-Takarli, and the three of them would read from a small book of Husain Mardan's. Their physical appearance conjured a state of neglect that reflected their fascination with existentialism: they wore cheap clothes and didn't shave. Desmond Stewart was a habitué of the Café Brazil. To the great delight of all, he was usually surrounded by young men listening to his translation of excerpts from Sartre's work.

64

Edmond al-Qushli became acquainted with existentialism before the al-Sadriya philosopher, but there's not a shred of proof that he influenced Abd al-Rahman, especially insofar as Edmond rejected existentialism decisively sometime around the end of the fifties or the beginning of the sixties. The two men met during the philosopher's return visits to Baghdad after his departure for Paris to study. It was after he learned of the affair between his cousin, Nadia Khaddouri, and the philosopher that al-Qushli rejected existentialism, colonialism, and capitalism. He thought up a new concept for rebellion, because he was neither moved to existentialism by the resistance nor satisfied by it, finding the philosophy to be effeminate, cowardly, quiet, and defeatist. Nadia distanced herself from him because her family had moved up in society and become part of the merchant class. Abd al-Rahman managed to win her because he was rich and belonged to the aristocracy, and Nadia's father was more interested in money than religion—what use was existentialism in this case? Edmond wanted a revolution, and this couldn't be an existential revolution because existentialism is not revolutionary. He wanted a sweeping Trotskyite revolution that would involve confusion, destruction, demolition, tearing away, and uprooting. There would doubtless be a revolution, one that he would lead. The first house he would destroy would be that of the bourgeois Abd al-Rahman, then the Khaddouri's. He would then proceed to annihilate one house at a time, one floor at a time. He would tie the members of those families with ropes, load them onto donkeys, and parade them before the people. Thanks to the revolution, he would be able to win Nadia, control her, and make her submit her to his sexual desires. He'd rape her, and it would be a Trotskyite rape. He'd win her over in an original way. He wouldn't say to her, "I adore you," but rather, "You're my revolution. You're the reward of those who struggle against colonialism, capitalism, and reactionaries. You'll be mine because you belong to me. You do not belong to the feudalists and the aristocrats."

This was the revolution that Edmond wanted to launch and which he planned, a revolution far removed from nausea, nihilism, and estrangement. But Nadia ended her relationship with Abd al-Rahman. He gave up on her and went to Paris, where he married a Frenchwoman, a relative of Sartre. The revolution toppled the Khaddouri family, and Nadia was attracted to the Trotsky of his time. He married her after the revolution, but he didn't rape her. Instead, he felt that he was being raped. This is how Edmond the Trotskyite befriended the bourgeois Khaddouri and both rallied against the philosopher of al-Sadriya.

The impoverished Elias Khaddouri worked making sweets in the Guarabed store owned by an Armenian merchant, while Faraj Khaddouri made straw baskets in Hasqeel Tawfiq's shop on the Murabba'a quarter. They lost their friends and had many detractors who made fun of them whenever they talked and shoved them on the stairs of the apartment building where they lived.

They moved to Yasin al-Khudayri's warehouse on Nazim Basha Street but didn't stay there long. The owner of the khan won them over with his kindness. They were extremely sensitive and in dire need of compassion. They expressed their appreciation for him through their love of work, and their affection increased whenever he forgave mistakes they made out of carelessness. He treated them with obvious deference, drinking with them on the balcony that overlooks the river and watching the sun set across the bridge.

After he went to London, where he chose to live, the Khaddouris were at the mercy of Abboud ibn Nazira, a harsh man who had plucked out the beard of the comic journalist Ibrahim Saleh Shukr because of a feuilleton he wrote that made fun of the government. They could not work in the atmosphere of imaginary plots he created and decided to leave. They went to Mahallet Qunbur Ali and rented a store and a small workshop, where they made rattan chairs.

Their pitiful financial state was obvious, and only through gargantuan efforts could they improve their lot. They worked day and night, and the situation slowly improved. After two years, owing to good work and trade ethics, they had achieved an acceptable financial status. The signs of wealth were apparent in their lives, and a number of posh shops opened around them, selling sweets, clothes, jewelry, shoes, and furniture. The most dramatic change happened after a deal they made with the business man Rick Dowell, a former British soldier in the first cavalry regiment that was led by Sir Frederick Maude, which entered Baghdad after the First World War.

66

Rick Dowell crossed the span that was later named Maude Bridge with the Sikh, Karka, and Gurkha soldiers occupying Baghdad in 1917, then proceeded to the palace in Mahallet Jadid Hasan Basha. He participated in the review of the British Army on al-Rashid Street, as can be seen in the one existing photograph of the event. Rick spent five years in Baghdad and did not return to London until the British troops withdrew, in the nineteen-twenties.

Rick returned to Baghdad after the Second World War to place flowers on the tombs of his friends, who were killed during the war of occupation, fighting against the Ottoman soldiers led by Khalil Pasha. He also visited the soldiers who were buried in the British cemetery near Bab al-Muadham. Elias and Faraj offered the ex-invader a beautiful chair made of the best rattan. This expression of generosity along with the wonderful welcome he received moved him to tears; he decided to sign a contract to export the finest of those oriental chairs upholstered with rugs to be sold in the Marks & Spencer store in London. The deal transformed the small atelier into a huge company with colored lighted billboards reading: "Khaddouri Company for the Export of Rattan Chairs."

Faraj and Elias were invited to exclusive parties with select guests. They became good friends with the Lawi family who owned car agencies on al-Rashid Street. Every Friday evening they went to parties organized by Sassoon Lawi. It was at one of those parties that Faraj fell in love with Elain Ifrayem, the most beautiful Jewess of her time.

Elain had a fair, youthful complexion very much like that of an Italian woman. She would move among reception guests with a cheerful face, wearing a white sleeveless blouse and short skirt. She exuded calm and joy. Faraj watched her while spreading butter on bread, feeling her presence immanently, letting his imagination run over her, and inhaling her scent whenever she came close. She melted at the slightest compliment or praise. She stood before him, neck straight, the contours of her chest visible under her well tailored clothes. The whole atmosphere of the illuminated reception hall and its warmth during the cold winter evenings augmented his awareness of Elain's femininity.

Elain was in love with Robin Assaf, who worked in the Guri medical supply depot. The Guri and Lawi families were enemies. Elain's family also considered Robin an adversary because he worked in their enemy's headquarters. They couldn't destroy or even harm Robin financially because he was already penniless, so they decided to ruin him socially, a strategy no one expected.

The elder Ifrayem, an accountant, knew that a person's worth was measured by the amount of money he possessed, which explains why he scratched Robin from the list of eligible suitors for Elain. Faraj was also an inappropriate match due to his religion. It was at that time that one of the sleaziest persons in Jewish circles, Mayer ben Nassim, the Lawi family accountant, appeared on the scene. Faraj Khaddouri paid Mayer a visit in his office to seek his help in his amorous schemes.

The office was filthy. Pistachio shells and cigarette butts cluttered the floor, and the place was disgusting. Mayer wore worn-out black clothes, the buttons were gone from his vest, his rugged wool shirt was stained with coffee, and his necktie was torn.

At the end of their long conversation Faraj was surprised to hear Mayer declare that there was an easy solution, "a simple trick."

"Yes my friend. It's easy," said Mayer, laughing. His face was fair and thin, his nose long, and his black eyes almost round. Smoothing his greasy hair with his hand, he explained his idea to Faraj. "Just give me a photograph, and I'll give you a fake Jewish birth certificate. It's easy my friend, very easy."

One of Butrus Samhiri's documents bore this description: "Mayer ben Nassim is a malicious Jew, a usurer, degenerate, and coward." The Lawi family and Mayer ben Nassim convinced Ifrayem that Faraj Khaddouri was a closet Jew. Faraj gave Ifrayem a lot of money for Elain's sake. He was willing to do anything to win Elain.

This is how the Lawi family was able to destroy their enemy socially. They humiliated and insulted him and forced him to run away to America a few days before Elain's wedding.

69

Elain converted to Christianity. The procession after her church wedding was led by a Chevrolet, a wedding gift from the Lawi family to Faraj, a down payment for his friendship and the price of his silence.

The procession of the newlyweds, preceded by gold-plated carriages, moved through al-Rashid Street, from the Plazia Restaurant to the Europe Palace Hotel on the Tigris River, where the newlyweds were spending one night before honeymooning in Venice, Rome, and Milan. Faraj enjoyed his wife's fair body under the Adriatic sun and returned home drunk with happiness.

The major change for the Khaddouri family was the location of their new house. They—Faraj and Elain, Elias and his wife Paulina, and their daughter Nadia—moved to al-Maarif Street, near the Armenian church.

The Khaddouri family chose to live in the outskirts of the city near the white palace where the king occasionally spent time. They built a large mansion, quite tall, surrounded by an impressive fence that separated it from the meadows and grazing animals. A huge garden featuring a fountain with a striped mosaic pattern facing the entrance of the house was the family's favorite gathering place in the evenings. The men smoked water pipes and the women happily sipped coffee with cardamom from porcelain cups.

Nadia changed as she made the transition from childhood to adolescence. Her expressions revealed a maturing young woman quite different from the capricious child she has been. She became kind and rather timid. In summer she slept until noon, and then went down to the garden, where her friends would join her. Sometimes she would ride in her father's car across the endless barley and lettuce fields. In winter she'd usually choose to stay home, near the fire, and feed it continuously. Occasionally she would visit Mayer's office, whose influence over her father was growing. He usually drove her back home or, with her father's approval, took her to the Plazia Restaurant for dinner. He had a permanent office room in the Khaddouri family business.

Nadia tried to emulate her father's goodheartedness and her mother's kindness and compassion. She wasn't gifted, but she was sensitive. She likely inherited her sensitivity from her father, and it is probably the only virtue she never lost.

Every day Nadia went to her father's company accompanied by the driver or Mayer ben Nassim. She often persuaded her father to have dinner with her at the Plazia Restaurant. Nadia usually chose a table near a window that looked out onto the street and would watch the passersby. She tried to be witty and entertaining, and when she grew tired of laughing she'd get up. Her father and Mayer would follow.

71

One day Nadia didn't get up at her usual time. Her father tried to get her out of bed, but she was feverish and didn't leave her room for two days. From that day on she never went back to her father's office, nor could she look Mayer in the face. Obviously disgusted, she was avoiding him. A year later Mayer left Baghdad for good, but Nadia was indelibly marked by her experience with that man.

72

After Mayer's departure Nadia began to lead a different kind of life. She was growing up and had matured considerably, especially after the Tigris River flooded. She devoted all her time to helping the victims. She and the maid would leave her house in the morning carrying a big pot of milk to distribute to the unfortunate people living in tents close to her house. She showed a great deal of compassion and was pained by their condition, the dangers that threatened them, and the poor conditions for the children in particular. This experience with the flood victims and her volunteer activities taught her the importance of work and the benefit of giving to others. A month later she told her parents that she wanted to look for a job outside the family business.

Surprised, her father asked, "Why do you want to work? Do you need money? You can have all the money you want."

But Nadia insisted, "No, no, I want to go out and be with people, I want to rely on myself."

Her mother had another explanation, "You must have been influenced by some silly notions." Nadia insisted, and three days later she found a job in the Mackenzie bookshop, where eventually she met the philosopher, who was on a family visit from Paris.

73

Nadia filled the house with joy whenever she came home for lunch. She ate with her father and took in the superb view of the greenery through the dining room window. Sometimes, even in the rain or wind, she would walk the dog on the grounds. She liked the sound of the wind and she loved the sight and smell of the orange blossoms.

She was not exactly happy, but at times she appeared to be exhilarated and at other times depressed—even on a beautiful day. She spent her weekends in the house relaxing in her favorite armchair, reading in the library, or simply staring into the flames in the fireplace.

74

The philosopher's relationship with Nadia lasted six months, from midsummer to midwinter. He was in Baghdad on a summer vacation after he had lost all hope of ever establishing a relationship with the waitress at the Café de Flore. He wanted to try his luck with Arab women, and to this end he frequented places where women usually gathered in large numbers. The moment he saw a woman he would begin fantasizing about her and imagine her naked in bed. This is how he'd assess her suitability. He'd imagine her fixing breakfast, putting on her house clothes, dressing up in eveningwear, then he'd decide on the degree of her appropriateness—in other words, whether she deserved the title of 'philosopher's wife.'

Abd al-Rahman enjoyed people's attention and their interest in him, a pleasure which clearly revealed the contradictions of his personality. There were times when he wanted to escape from himself and his loneliness and be with other people. And then there were times when he wanted, in compliance with his philosophical orientation, to show indifference and disinterest in others. But everything in the world worked against him.

The philosopher was well aware of the presence of two distinct worlds in his life—the deep internal world, where philosophy reigned, and the external world of easy, practical matters. Finding a compromise between the two and bridging their differences was no small feat. Here arose the ambiguity of marrying an Arab woman: How could one marry a woman who was neither an existentialist nor versed in any philosophy at all?

Abd al-Rahman's imagination responded to his dilemma during the first month of his visit to Iraq. He would sit in the living room of his parents' house, stare into the dense gardens, and imagine himself invisible, strongly convinced that somewhere there was a women for him, a woman capable of understanding his philosophy, of understanding him, and singling him out from a sea of philosophers. The man he saw in his mind would have a tired-looking face, thoughtful eyes, calm hand movements, and a certain dreaminess born of the misery and nihilism of existence.

Sometimes he considered this issue childish and even stupid, especially when he began visiting his relatives and observed the behavior of the young women. They would sit up straight with legs crossed and heads bowed, looking at the floor as a sign of subservience. He despised this attitude, all the foolishness of courting, the love notes, the successes and failures. He considered them a waste of a philosopher's time and a distraction from his meditation. One day, before he had decided when he would return to Paris, he went to the Mackenzie bookshop.

75

Nadia attracted the philosopher's attention. He noticed her among the other shy, sad-looking women. She stood out in her print dress, a flower in her hair, her soft, calm voice and Christian accent. She was different from the other girls he knew, who idly stayed home and quietly worked on their embroidery. Abd al-Rahman felt that she would be able to share his experience, since when he said Sartre, she responded, "I know him. I know his book, *La nausée*. It costs 200 fils. We have it in the store." He mentioned Camus, and she responded right away, "I know him; he wrote a novel entitled *L'etranger*. It costs either 150 or 200 fils. I can't remember."

So she knew them all, Suhail Idris, Aida Matraji Idris, Dar al-Adab, and Simone de Beauvoir. Even if she only knew the price of their books, that counted for something. This was not an easy matter. No one among the existentialists of the world would know the price of books on existentialism. She'd be an asset for his philosophy. She'd be able to provide the price of philosophy and its cost overseas. Another woman would have asked stupidly, "Sartre? Who is this Sartre?" Whenever he went into the bookstore and looked at the books on the shelves, tired of his nausea, he would see her, as part of the colored book covers; he would visualize her live image and Sartre's picture on the same cover. This image swelled his affection for her. She was, in his mind, a part of the books on the shelves. His presence and mood always affected her deeply as well. His power undermined her self-control, and she had to rein in her emotions. Nonetheless, she always conducted herself properly.

He would often spend a couple of hours in the bookstore, checking over the books, reading, and looking for a title he wanted. There were moments when their eyes would meet and she felt drawn to him. Her emotions imparted a certain feminine charm to her face that strongly attracted him. Whenever she asked him, "You read a lot, don't you?"

"I do," he'd respond. "I'm a philosopher."

This marked the beginning of the philosopher's affair with Nadia Khaddouri, and the end of Edmond al-Qushli's connection with existentialism and his shift toward Trotskyism.

76

Edmond loved Nadia deeply. Whenever he visited her he would wait a few minutes before going into the house. As soon as he saw her, he would freeze until she took his hand and tugged him gently inside the house. He was a tall man, and his head reached the crystal chandelier in the living room. A picture of the Virgin Mary hung over the fireplace near a display of silver rosaries. An icon of Christ and an incense burner were on a table. On a mahogany shelf a New Testament was left open to the page where Nadia had been reading.

On one of his visits to Nadia's house, looking at the open Bible, he asked, without looking at her "Do you read the New Testament?"

"Every day," she replied. Her long chestnut hair fell over her shoulders, and her naked arms were as white as cotton.

That day Nadia was wearing a tight skirt that revealed her shapely legs. Her face was beautiful, pure, and pleasing as she looked into her cousin's eyes. He berated her strongly, "You're a Christian, and you love a Muslim!" She said nothing, but she wasn't embarrassed and looked away as if thinking of something else. He pressed on: "You're in love, aren't you?"

"I thought you didn't differentiate between Christians and Muslims," she retorted.

"What about you," he asked. "Don't you draw a difference?"

"When I am in love, I don't differentiate," she said, "Love does not differentiate."

He continued talking, his eyes moist, "I usually don't discriminate, but when I fall in love I do." He looked around the room and examined its contents, then got up and left, fighting back tears. Nadia was silent. She was sad, and as soon as the front door closed behind Edmond, she heard him break down. Moved, she sat on the chair where he had sat and she cried too.

77

Abd al-Rahman was mesmerized by Nadia when he saw her for the first time. Though she didn't wear glasses, as he liked women to do, he couldn't take his eyes off the snug clothes that molded her body and the distinctive paleness of her face, which was free of any haughtiness or oppression. He liked her calm self-confidence as well as her constant efforts to inveigle and impress him.

He didn't mind her occasionally abrasive reactions, jokes, and allusions or her cool, reserved mien. On the contrary, these characteristics of hers piqued his interest, though they didn't add to her sexual attraction for him. She was a little stiff and determined, firm even—qualities he liked because they set her apart from the prostitutes he had known in Paris. In a sense, she presented him with a field for discovery, a venue for adventure, a gamble, or an object to be captured and possessed. But he wanted to reach an objective opinion, one grounded in philosophical wisdom and logic without losing himself.

One day, sipping orange juice and laughing, Nadia winked at him as he was considering his options with her. She was trying to lick a drop of juice from her lower lip. He loved the way she pulled back her lips and closed her mouth without causing a stir.

Nadia perplexed him from the moment he first saw her. He couldn't resist being attracted to her, but it wasn't easy for him to engage her. She exhausted him with her affected reserve. Whenever he let himself go, she'd crush him with her charm, the same charm that had defeated Edmond before him. He was sapped by her naive sweetness. She provoked strange reactions in him. He was ready to believe anything she said and felt that she was scheming to control his heart.

He explained to her the importance of philosophy and insisted that he was not so naive as to believe that God had created the nose as a perch for glasses or that the feet were meant only for socks, or even that human beings were merely bait for Death. He told her about the theory of cause and effect, citing the example of a sailor who loses his teeth as a result of scurvy.

Abd al-Rahman was unable to hide his love for her, and with his love came jealousy. He adored her and, utterly helpless, surrendered to her every wish. He was convinced that he had to marry her because, simply put, she understood his philosophy and his wisdom; in other words, there was total harmony between him and her wisdom, her nature, and her ability to understand philosophy and put up with him. Based on his conviction that God created everything to serve him, he believed that she was the creature that God had intended for him. This thinking reflected his belief that he was the center of the universe.

The philosopher was well aware that love affairs do not end peacefully—or at least not the way he wanted them to end, simply and happily. He had to be extremely careful in setting out on this adventure and was even considering taking special precautions to end the affair at precisely the right time. Otherwise, what would differentiate him from ordinary people? He'd have to review the lives of all famous people, from Sartre to the hero of Brand Brooks adventure stories.

He needed love, and this time things were going well. His conscience bothered him only slightly. He was enjoying himself a great deal, free of the pain he had suffered in his pursuit of the Café de Flore waitress. His enjoyment possibly even exceeded the limited pleasures provided by Paris prostitutes. This love didn't make him anxious but proceeded smoothly, like crossing a bridge, and was fired by the occasional nod or a smile when he left the bookshop.

The first time they went out, Abd al-Rahman took Nadia on a circuit of Baghdad. They went to the cinema and the Orient Express café and ended the tour in a well-known restaurant. She didn't say a word the whole time and was somewhat moody. He didn't appreciate her attitude and was about to lose his temper, having chatted the whole time about philosophy. He wanted her to know that there was a philosophy based on talk and that talking was a kind of purging that brings a perfect happiness. It was an art, the art of chatting with a beautiful young woman like her.

78

Nadia and her mother Helen were invited to Mrs. Adileh's, in the Hasan Pasha district, to celebrate Easter. The young women of the house received them warmly, but Edmond was not there. Grandma Adileh's living room displayed signs of her faith, such as the image of the Virgin Mary on the wall and the cross above the door. Samaan, Edmond's uncle, was praying and sprinkling the house with holy water he had brought from the church. The smell of incense filled the house.

Umm Butrus was cleaning the windows, and her daughter was moving among the guests with a tray of sweets and nuts. The chatter of the young women, their soft laughter, and their high voices echoed throughout the house. The guests included many relatives — Aida and Georgette, Samaan's daughters; Edmond's cousin Nadia; Helen, Nadia's uncle's wife; and Anisa and Salwa, the daughters of Hanna Qushli. Friends and neighbors were there too: Marroki's wife Suzan, also Jenna, Fladya, Amira, and others. Even their Muslim and Jewish neighbors were invited: Rahmeh; Hamdiya; Suad, the daughter of the former chief of police; Miyya, daughter of Abd al-Qader al-Mumayyez; Rafla al-Dawdi; and Karna Ajas, the pharmacist's daughter. Their jewelry twinkled in the candlelight.

Suddenly Edmond entered. He immediately noticed Nadia, who was radiant with her beautiful skin, her fine figure, and her delicate fingers illuminated by the lights. He greeted each young woman with an affected smile, but when he stood before Nadia he felt his heart was about to break. Nadia had lowered her head to look at a book, and her eyelashes cast a slight shadow onto her cheeks. He greeted her with a reproach: "Hello Nadia, it has been a long time since you last visited Grandma Adileh!" Nadia did not reply.

Her transparent skin, well-drawn nose, and the twinkle in her almond-shaped eyes disturbed Edmond. Standing before her, he didn't know what to do with himself. After a few seconds of hesitation he grabbed a plate of sweets and offered her some. She took a piece, opened her mouth wide to avoid smearing her lipstick, and then dipped her fingers into a glass filled with rosewater. He handed her his white handkerchief to dry her fingers, took it back when she was finished, and went to his room. There he sat facing Trotsky's photograph and broke into tears. He was devastated to see Sartre triumph over Trotsky and could not bear the idea of Abd al-Rahman sauntering about the streets of Baghdad with Nadia, spending time with her in restaurants, enjoying her company.

79

Abd al-Rahman started going to the Mackenzie bookshop every day and watched Nadia from behind the glass while smoking his pipe. Nadia often put pink ribbons in her hair and wore a print dress with small flowers. He couldn't take his eyes off her. He scrutinized her every move and wanted to hold her very tight, as if he would never see her again. They used to meet every day after work at the Orient Express café near Maude Bridge, drink coffee, and talk for a couple hours. Edmond was aware of Abd al-Rahman's daily visits to the Mackenzie bookshop. He couldn't stand the thought of their daily encounters and growing intimacy. He would have loved to be the one watching Nadia from behind the glass, basking in her beauty.

On their third outing Abd al-Rahman tried to kiss her, but she refused. He pulled her to him, but she was trembling and had tears in her eyes. Her heart was beating fast and she put him off, saying in a hoarse voice, "No, no—I can't." He asked her for an explanation while still trying to touch her soft thigh under the table. She pushed him away. "I don't know why, but things like that are repulsive to me. There was an incident . . . ."

"What sort of incident?!" exclaimed Abd al-Rahman.

"I can't . . . I can't," she said, and fled the table.

He stood facing her. She was surprised and agitated, convinced that he had spoiled their relationship by dredging up a painful memory and doubting her. He left the café and walked beside her quietly down al-Rashid Street. They talked and slowly regained their usual familiarity, walking so close that their bodies almost touched. He liked to impress Nadia with talk about existentialism, nausea, estrangement, nihilism, and the absurd. For her part, she liked this abstractness that kept their focus distracted from physical matters. She liked this philosopher's inclination toward delusive imagination, a yearning for the forbidden, and the ability to create great works in the air. Abd al-Rahman liked to walk in front of her and look at her as he continued talking nonstop, while she chimed, "A great philosopher."

Abd al-Rahman felt that his love for her was stronger and deeper than her love for him. He never imagined that love could be so deep and catch a person so unawares. He disliked her calm, which bordered on aloofness. He was convinced that love proceeded according to inviolable but mysterious rules that impelled him to meld into her with all due force.

The philosopher wanted Nadia always to focus on him, admire him, and appreciate his greatness. Every time he talked to her about his successful philosophical debates with the greatest western philosophers he never failed to ask, "Well, what do you think of me?" She always replied, "A great philosopher."

The things that Abd al-Rahman feared most were neglect, estrangement, and betrayal. He had a limitless ability to listen to comments about his greatness. He also knew that love was madness, and he believed exclusively in lust and sex. That's why Nadia's reserved attitude was suffocating him and put him off. He wanted her to pine for him and him alone. He became obsessed with this wish, and this obsession affected his behavior. He was obliged to take solace in words in order not to push her against the fence of the Armenian Church, press his body hard against hers, and force her to submit to him.

Nadia was not the innocent girl she seemed to be. She endured an excruciating inner struggle, torn between her physical desires and the memory she couldn't erase. She wanted to resolve this conundrum using the philosopher as bait, and she enjoyed tormenting him. She considered him vulnerable, an antihero. She found Abd al-Rahman weak and consumed by his imagination, and she only pretended to believe him and his endless truth-defying proclamations. Of course, he never doubted that she believed him. She knew that this was his nature and that he was quick to cry or laugh. He was nothing but a contradiction caught between happiness and a mirage that existed solely in his imagination. She was well aware that he had a mind that roamed freely, a result of his obsessions, delusions, pains, failures, and denial.

Abd al-Rahman wanted his yearnings and memories to be firmly anchored to her, but after he took her home he was usually sad and frazzled because their conversations had not led to sex. He was left feeling empty. He realized that becoming a destructive existentialist through the application of continuous chatting was a myth. He felt nauseated, having strayed from his true self by getting involved in something alien and then gradually having lost his identity. He would stand near the lemon tree in his father's garden, calling up a single repulsive image of her that he resented and from which he wanted to free himself. He had longed to kiss her and desired, more than anything, to simply take her, but the cell of existence was pressing too tight around him. In order to expunge her, he avidly sought a connection to some other world, a world without limits that he could interpose between himself and her notions of separation and defensiveness. He wanted to leave her to deal with indifference, to cast her far away, but he didn't know how.

He desired her, but he felt disgusted by the idea of marrying her because he didn't want to pass the futility of life—by means of a struggle in bed—to another human being who experienced unhappiness and suffering similar to his own. He liked depravity, which he felt was close to his soul. It was a renewal of his thinking and imagination, a taboo he pondered, a thirst for a special sort of worship, a type of isolation, a fulfillment that no one knew but which was cheap, enjoyable, and forbidden. It liberated him from his depraved dreams and freed him from pimples and nervous illnesses, the hatred of the body as a malady of existence. It freed him from dislikes, the disappointments of life, and its shortcomings.

He was at a loss as he stood in his parents' garden, not know-ing what to do next. He suddenly raised his head and saw a black cat at the window. He ran after it with a broom and swore at it, uttering words that are not fit to repeat. His true anger was aimed at Nadia, not the cat. She was the real threat to his existence.

When he returned to his room he decided to get drunk. He poured whiskey in a glass, added ice, and began to read Nizar Qabbani's poems. He started reading the poem entitled, "Existentialism," which discusses two aspects of existentialism in Paris. The poet saw his beloved's eyes tear for the gray Parisian sky, he heard the whispers of her long throat, he visualized her hair cut à la garcon, and remembered the color of her dress. He imagined her dancing to the sound of jazz and the birds' song, and saw her walking in a narrow Parisian street. Qabbani recalled how lively she used to be, how eagerly she chose the first thing she saw, her burning love for life as he was listening to the incessant barking of the dog. Abd al-Rahman couldn't get over this shock. The winding path of love, spiraling like a snail. Love made him feel pain and joy at the same time. Despite his resentment, he was eager to see her the next morning.

He went to the bookshop and stood in front of her, unkempt and two days unshaven. She was impeccable, reflecting the ele-gance of a person in love. Her hair was beautifully coiffed, her makeup perfect, her face blooming, and her perfume filling the shop. She wore a red coat and a matching silk scarf. Her beauty and elegance were irresistible. He was speechless and cast about in vain for a topic of conversation. He was increasingly aware of her hold on him—a prisoner of her charm, unable to escape and save himself. The matter was out of his hands. He told her calmly, "I love you and I want to marry you."

Her answer came fast and loud, "Please. We are in a place of work. Sartre's books are on the last shelf." He was instantly aware of the banality of the scene: A lover goes to an angry mistress and says one word to her; she shouts at him that they are in a workplace and directs him to the object of his interest to give customers the impression that he was pestering her. She then threatens to have him thrown out if he oversteps his boundaries again.

The following day he told her that he did not love her because she did not love him. They were sitting in the Orient Express café watching the rain from behind the glass. Nadia cried and covered her eyes, but he didn't believe her. He knew this was a classic trick between lovers. He told her, "I've decided to leave you and go back to Paris." When she looked up, her eyes were filled with tears and her cheeks were red. She turned her face to look at the passersby and saw people with umbrellas running through the rain. In the crowd a young couple laughed and held hands as the rain fell on their faces.

Abd al-Rahman thought that she would return to him easily, but her continued silence made him aware that he was being overbearing. His ploy had not worked, and he knew he'd made a big mistake. The waiter placed newspapers on their table alongside their coffee. The philosopher tried to change her mind, but it was soon evident that nothing he said would help. Nadia got up and left without looking back. He took his coat, left money on the table, and ran after her. She was walking fast, unconcerned by him or the rain that fell on her face and made her makeup run. He followed her and tried to talk, but she ignored him. Around them people were waiting to enter the cinemas and cafés; the smell of grilled meat filled the air in al-Rashid Street.

Abd al-Rahman was completely shocked and in denial. He thought she was bluffing, and he tried to ignore her, but she didn't change her mind and went home. He realized that he couldn't get from her what she didn't want to give. Nadia had reduced him to his true size and had preserved her dignity. When he turned his back on her she turned her back on him. He was well aware now that there was no use being stubborn.

Rain was falling heavily when he arrived home. He rushed past his parents in the living room without saying a word and went directly to his room. He sat facing Sartre's photograph and cried bitterly. He didn't believe in Nadia anymore, and he was convinced that his love for her would end up destroying him. But soon the pain caused by his failed love changed into happiness as he realized that true love and true philosophy overcome everything. He was not only crazy about existentialism, he was also eager to assimilate its principles and strongly oppose anyone who denounced them.

Abd al-Rahman decided to join his parents downstairs, even if this meant revealing to everybody that he was hurting and had just had a falling-out with his sweetheart. He sat in a comfortable armchair, looked around the splendidly furnished room, and said to himself, "Here, I can read Jean-Paul Sartre's books." He looked through the large window covered with raindrops and suddenly remembered a fishmonger he had met in Paris. One cold day the fishmonger had tried to cover his ears with a very thick hat. Abd al-Rahman transposed Sartre's face onto that of the fishmonger's and imagined Sartre as a fisherman with Simone de Beauvoir at his side eating a cookie. When Sartre tugged the fishing rod, there was an explosion and Sartre melted into the water like a piece of ice. Simone de Beauvoir was left standing alone, feeling deeply saddened by Sartre's sudden disappearance.

80

During his courtship of Nadia, Abd al-Rahman had made various attempts to get physically closer to her by stealing a kiss or letting his hand wander onto her thigh, but Nadia objected very strongly. When he asked for an explanation she told him that one day she would send him a letter and explain her attitude in writing. In the meantime, he was flooding her with boring letters that were filled with phony grievances and put-on anger. He wrote these letters in the hope of frightening her and prompting her to write him love letters that were overflowing with affection. He wanted to uncover her secret, the reason for her strong reaction to his attempted kiss. One day she finally sent him that letter.

81

I was not able to locate the letter Nadia Khaddouri wrote to the al-Sadriya philosopher, even though many other documents confirmed its existence. That letter led to their breakup. It was reported to me that after reading the letter Abd al-Rahman shouted so loudly that the whole household was alarmed and everybody rushed to his room, to find a totally broken man. No one could confirm to me whether the two of them met after that letter, but some people assured me that he chased her everywhere she went before finally leaving for Paris. He never talked to her, however, but rather watched her from a distance and saw the signs of sadness and pain on her face.

When he again returned to Baghdad he was married to Germaine, a plain Parisian girl whom he passed off as Sartre's cousin.

82

Abd al-Rahman was extremely agitated and was unable to distinguish clearly between his inner feelings and the strange ideas that crossed his mind. He packed his bags and left for Paris. No one knew how Nadia truly felt afterward, but she had left her work at the bookstore and stayed home. She was seen only once outside the house, helping the victims of the explosion at al-Kilani power station, which happened a few days after the revolution. The victims had set up their tents close to her father's house. She regularly distributed food to them and played with their children. Those who saw her reported that her experience with Abd al-Rahman had not diminished her beauty. Five months later Edmond proposed to her.

83

Edmond was nervous as he walked toward Nadia's house. She greeted him and was extremely surprised by the change in Edmond's appearance: his vest, white shirt, carefully combed hair, and a Trotskyite beard together transformed him into an attractive young man.

They sat facing each other with their knees nearly touching. The warm ambiance and the beauty of the place helped Edmond relax. He took out his pipe and searched for his tobacco, but Nadia offered him some of her father's tobacco. Both felt at ease and looked lovingly into each other's eyes. Edmond was emboldened and began toying with Nadia's cross. She did not object and moved closer to him and when he kissed her she responded. It was the kiss that Abd al-Rahman had so longed for.

84

Among all the documents I had was a single photograph showing Edmond and Nadia together. It was a very important picture, but I couldn't confirm whether it was taken before or after the wedding. They looked elegant, attractive, and young, and one couldn't help but find them appealing. I found that photograph in the archives of the photographer Hazem Pack.

There is no doubt however that Nadia and Edmond were married. The documents refer to the wedding, the church where it was celebrated, and the first night they spent in the Khaddouri house. On the morning after their wedding the servants heard Edmond vow to kill Abd al-Rahman.

85

That morning Nadia came down from her room feeling agitated and nervous and she pretended to busy herself arranging the flowers. Edmond followed, looking sad, and sat on the sofa facing her. He was disheveled, his beard uncombed, and he smoked nervously. He went to Nadia, held her by the shoulders, and shouted at her, "Liar, liar!" He couldn't control himself and was barely able to stand upright. He repeated, "Liar! You're not a virgin!" Nadia kept quiet and turned her face away from him. Edmond wouldn't stop. "It must have been Abd al-Rahman. He did it to you. It's him! Say it." But Nadia vehemently denied the accusation.

Edmond pushed Nadia to the floor; he wanted to crush her fingers with his foot and beat her. She defended herself as best she could, crying. Edmond kept accusing Abd al-Rahman of deflowering her. She denied it, swearing in the name of Christ that Abd al-Rahman was not responsible, but to no avail. Finally she said, "It was not him, but someone else. It was Mayer ben Nassim, when I was a girl." He didn't believe her, but she went on explaining and trying to exonerate Abd al-Rahman. "I swear it was Mayer. I wrote a letter to Abd al-Rahman and explained that I was not a virgin, but he ran away to Paris. This is the whole truth." Edmond was still not convinced.

"I don't believe you. It is this cowardly existentialist, this base fellow who did it. Just be patient, and I, Edmond son of Adileh, will wash away this dishonor and take my revenge."

86

That evening Faraj, Elias Khaddouri, and Edmond held serious discussions to decide what action must be taken. The servants saw them, and two of them swore to me that they heard the three men talk about killing Abd al-Rahman in an act of vengeance. I met those two servants, Boulos and his sister Malakin, in their house in Camp Sarah near the Zahleh markets. They passed this information on to me, but I couldn't confirm that this incident was behind the death of one of Iraq's greatest philosophers of the sixties. Nor did any of the documents I had confirmed this as a possibility. A document provided by Sadek Zadeh maintains that the philosopher committed suicide. A possible scenario can be based on the following reasoning: Abd al-Rahman's physical and mental condition was deteriorating, which might have led him to have a nervous breakdown, and end his life with a self-inflicted gunshot. I could imagine him thinking about the millions of people who went about their business with vulgar enthusiasm but without seizing the essence of life, and wanting to set an example for them. Before killing himself he would have felt everything around him was nauseating, and that the objects in his room were closing in on him. He took a gun from a drawer and pointed it calmly at his chest. Germaine had just come out of the bathroom when she heard the shot. She ran to his room and shouted from behind the locked door, "What have you done, what have you done?" The servants broke the door down and found him lying on the floor with one red spot on the left side of his chest.

87

Naturally, this scenario needed to be verified. It was meant to convince us that nausea and nihilism as an aspect of life—and not its nonexistence (the Iraqi intellectuals of the time did not differentiate between the two)—were the reasons for the philosopher's suicide. But I had my doubts, because for the al-Sadriya philosopher nausea motivated him to embrace life, not to reject it. It was a way to shout out against the stillness of life, and an incentive for an enthusiastic approach to it, rather than a reason for asceticism and the torture of the body. I had to go beyond this document that Sadeq Zadeh described as the most important.

I had to verify a second theory: the Trotskyite conspiracy. It was suggested as the Khaddouri family sat in their garden, near the fountain one afternoon, together with Edmond and Elain, drinking tea and eating cookies. "Let's kill him," said Edmond, biting into his cookie.

"No," said Elain in her Jewish accent, "we need to do something that won't leave evidence." Nadia's mother wondered how this could be accomplished, and Elain explained, "We need to create a scandal."

Faraj approved wholeheartedly: "Excellent idea!"

88

Ismail went to meet Edmond at his house on Anastas al-Karmali Street. Edmond met him at the door and took him to a table filled with a variety of foods worthy of a banquet: fish, chicken, many kinds of sweets, fruits, flatbread, and plenty of whiskey. The conversation turned around the life of the poor and the revolution that had brought down the bourgeoisie, feudalism, and the Sirkaliya system.

When Ismail left Edmond's house he was totally drunk and staggering. His eyes twinkled as he examined the boxes of sweets his host had given him.

89

Soon after his meeting with Edmond, Ismail started visiting the philosopher's wife while her husband was absent. A week before his death Abd al-Rahman told his wife that he would not be spending the night at home, but she didn't seem to care and went on washing her young daughter's face.

Ismail arrived after midnight, and when he learned that her husband was absent he decided to stay with Germaine until dawn. They ate and drank, and as he was about to leave she asked him to go with her, naked, up to the roof.

90

She was elated, and when she reached the roof she lay down on the bed. Ismail did the same. They resumed their lovemaking to the sound of music under the clear summer sky. They felt they were on another planet far from the struggles of daily life.

The minaret of the Siraj al-Din Mosque was close to the house and quite high. Germaine said to Ismail, "Look at the minaret. It's as if someone is watching us." He laughed, looked at the minaret and then the empty street, where only a barking dog and the whistle of the guard could be heard, and reassured her, "No, the imam won't watch us." Germaine got up, covered herself with a sheet, and looked at the courtyard of the mosque. She saw a tree bearing small fruit hidden from passersby by the high wall. She turned to Ismail, ran her fingers across his body and said, "I want one of these apples." Ismail was surprised but he complied. He put on his black trousers and went down to the courtyard. As soon as the guard moved away, he climbed the tree and picked as many green apples as he could. When he heard someone coming down the minaret's steps, he quickly hid the apples in his pants, and clambered down. Two hands grabbed him immediately, one by the neck and the other by his pants. It was the imam, who exulted, "I've caught you, sinner." The guard came over, and by the light of the moon he saw Ismail's pants filled with the mosque's apples. Ismail's pleas for mercy went unheeded. The guard, proud and happy to have finally caught a scofflaw, shouted at him, "You are a thief, and you steal from a mosque!"

The imam added, "He is also an adulterer."

When Ismail sought to correct him, "Only a thief," the imam pronounced, "I was watching you from the minaret. You delayed my call to prayer, you sinners."

Hoping to confound him, Ismail suggested, "Maybe you were watching a porn flick, imam?"

The guard didn't like Ismail's rudeness. He told him to take off his pants, leaving him totally naked, and tied him to a tree. Meanwhile the imam had climbed the minaret and invited the inhabitants of al-Sadriya to come and see the adulterer.

All this took place as Germaine, covered only with a sheet, watched, helpless and mortified, from her roof.

91

The scandal must have been more than Abd al-Rahman could handle. The documents confirm that he died one week after the news broke of his wife's liaison with his colleague. His life turned upside down; Germaine returned to Paris; Ismail disappeared; Edmond immigrated to Australia; and no one knew what happened to Nadia. Was this the Trotskyite plot hatched by Edmond and Ismail? Did Ismail betray Abd al-Rahman on his own? Was he, a betrayer by nature, pushed to do so? Was it the wife who wanted to cheat on a husband busy with his nausea, his dissolute life, and the prostitutes in the nightclubs?

It was up to me to answer all these questions and finish up the philosopher's biography I had started writing three months earlier. I had been working on it nonstop, totally involved in it, in order to receive the money promised to me by Hanna Yusif and Nunu Behar.

The Philosopher's Journey

One quiet morning, having almost finished the philosopher's biography, I woke up early and pulled open the curtains of the casement overlooking the street. I opened the window and felt the cold air hit my face. The sun was pale, and its rays spread over the upper stories of the buildings, hotels, and luxurious houses. The smell of ink reminded me of the drama of lost-love stories I had lived with ever since I had dived into the maze of documents in search of the words that gradually formed themselves into the stories of real people.

Those words shaped the philosopher's distorted hands, his large, handsome chest, and sleepy look. They put some order into the flurry of documents that encumbered my desk and my room, and inspired the writing of the biography: there were documents, old newspapers, magazines thrown everywhere, piles of rough copies, and photographs. The furniture in the apartment was covered with dust. My dog barked nonstop after I tied him to the bedpost with my belt to prevent him from disturbing the papers or breaking the pens. There were leftover bits of food: dark bread crusts that looked like a stain on the table, an open bag, and the remains of a hard-boiled egg.

Writing freed me of all that because I could give free rein to the emotions the philosopher was unable to express. I revived him, breathed life into him, brought him to the brink of an explosion. By this I don't mean I wrote a book of history; I always insisted on the danger and futility of an interpretation based on history. No, I made room for imagination and a place for his personality in the biography, filling the gap between the imagined personality and the real subject. What the flesh-and-blood philosopher and the philosopher on paper have in common is the way of life, the environment, and the persons that surround them. I became aware that people live only through their imagined selves, which led me to establish a relationship between words and objects through the imagination of the characters and their delusions. I created a supplementary image in the mind, one that was more anguished in the abstract than it was in reality. It is an image that a work written without sincere concern for the main character cannot include between its covers.

As I said earlier, I was looking at the street from the window, and I saw a woman carrying a bag, a nightingale taking in the cold of the gardens. Then I heard the thin sound of a violin wafting on the fresh air, entering my room through the window, and spreading like a long, well-combed beard.

I drew a bath and jumped into the tub to relax after a strenuous period of work. I closed my eyes and let myself go, enjoying the scent of the salts I had put in the water. Suddenly I heard a noise that sounded as if someone were trying to break into my apartment. The dog was barking, and I was petrified, as if my body had turned into a log floating in the bathwater. I slid out of the tub, put on my bathrobe, and half-opened the door. Hanna Yusif was moving surreptitiously toward my desk. I went out and asked him what he was doing in my apartment. It was a silly question because I knew very well that he was after the philosopher's biography. He was startled and tried to hide his embarrassment. He laughed loudly, "Oh! You're here! I didn't know, forgive me." When I asked him how he managed to open the door, he pulled a ring of keys from his pocket and said, "I opened it with the key, believe me. I found those keys in my pocket and said to myself, let me try one of them."

"You should have knocked," I shouted.

"By Christ, I did knock, but you didn't hear me. I thought you weren't at home, and I decided to come in and wait for you," he explained.

I rejected his excuse, "Hanna, when I am not at home you do not have permission to come in. You know this. It's simple good manners!"

He continued to defend himself. "I know, but we're friends — or I thought we were."

The dog was stretched out near the bed, sweating, his eyes yellowish. His mouth was opening and closing, his teeth were not showing. I was alarmed and went to check his pulse. Hanna said, "Don't worry. He won't die. It's a temporary anesthetic. He'll come back to his senses in a few minutes." The dog was moaning and twitching slowly on the floor. I went to my room to get dressed, and when I returned I saw Hanna going through my papers on the table.

I went to the kitchen to make coffee, and I heard Hanna laugh as he was reading the papers. He was more elegant this day than when I first saw him. He carried a silver cane and used it for appearances only. He wore a shiny blazer and a vest with a silver watch in one of the pockets. His hair was well combed, and his cologne filled the space of the room. All this elegance, however, could not hide his depravity and hypocrisy.

I put his coffee on the table, and when I turned to look at him, his hand was shaking. He said to me, "I'll take these papers home to read." I objected, "No, Hanna. I have not completed my work yet."

The truth is that I had made two copies of my biography. One I hid in my clothes closet, and the other was on the desk. I was worried about the future and didn't trust Hanna Yusif or Sadeq Zadeh. I was able to persuade Hanna to read the papers in my apartment.

I went out to eat breakfast and buy cigarettes and left Hanna in the apartment to read. I hurried back and found him tearing up some of the pages and dumping them in the wastebasket. I shouted at him, "What are you doing!" He explained, "Nothing, some of the information is incorrect, believe me." He had destroyed all the pages on which I wrote of the suicide of the philosopher but showed a great interest in the activities of Ismail Hadoub. He was more interested in this character than in the others. Laughing indecently, he said he wanted me to provide more dirt about Ismail. His malicious eyes moved from page to page. Finally he agreed, "What you've written is enough. Can I take the biography home with me?"

"Yes, you may, once you pay me the agreed upon wage." But he wasn't prepared for that.

"I'll give you your money tomorrow. I didn't expect you to finish it so soon. Believe me, I'll pay you tomorrow." But I insisted and told him that he wouldn't get the biography before he gave me the money he owed me.

I took great pleasure in tormenting him. He would first beg me to accede to his request, and whenever he failed he'd act as if it didn't matter to him. He'd seem to give up, "OK, I'll leave it here then, even though we've agreed that I'll pay you. Don't worry. I'll give your money. I can't deny you your rights. You've worked very hard the whole time."

Then he'd flip the pages and come up with another reason to take the manuscript home, "If you give it to me today I'll correct some of the historical mistakes and give it back to you for a rewrite, then I could pay you. Once you're done with the corrections, I'll come back with Nunu Behar and take the final version."

I thought to myself, "what's wrong with giving him this copy? I have another one. I can discover his intentions from the historical corrections he wants to make." I told him, "All right Hanna, take these papers with you on condition that you return them to me tomorrow with the money." He could hardly contain himself. He snatched up the manuscript and fairly flew out of the apartment.

I began straightening up my apartment and placing the documents in their place in the cupboard. I discovered that some documents related to Ismail Hadoub's life had disappeared. Frantic, I looked for them everywhere—under my papers, between the magazines and newspapers, under the bed. I was looking among my clothes when I heard a knock. Sadeq Zadeh and Nunu Behar were at the door. Sadeq pushed me inside and asked, "What did you give Hanna?"

"Nothing," I said, fully aware of my lie. Sadeq was furious and his eyes were spewing flame.

"Where is the biography?" asked Nunu. I opened my cupboard and gave them the second copy. They leafed through it while I watched, seated beside my dog.

Nunu Behar sat on a chair holding her purse while Sadeq Zadeh read through the philosopher's biography, commenting volubly. "Not true. I never said that! Liar, liar." He was swearing and whistling his fury, then turned to me, "Where did you get these documents?"

"Which documents," I asked, frightened by the tone of his voice.

"The documents related to Ismail Hadoub." I was silent and nervous. I had never expected Ismail Hadoub's story to be more important than the philosopher's. I was commissioned to write a biography of the philosopher not of Ismail Hadoub, and if I included information about him it was because he augmented the image of the philosopher. I said to Sadeq, "But you told me that the most important thing was to write about the philosopher's life. I don't understand this sudden interest in Ismail Hadoub."

Sadeq couldn't restrain himself. He jumped nervously from his seat, grabbed me by the neck with one hand, and held a gun to my head with the other. Fuming, he growled, "You wrote the biography of the philosopher because we paid you to do so, but who asked you to write about Ismail Hadoub? What obscene person induced you to do it? Tell me!"

I defended myself, "No one told me to do it, but I found that Ismail was important for understanding the personality of the philosopher, believe me."

Nunu Behar tried to calm him down. "Leave him, Ismail. Let him be." Until this second I had not realized that Sadeq was Ismail Hadoub. I hadn't written about him to expose him, and if he had told me the truth I would have embellished his image. If only to spare myself his wrath and to get my money I would have avoided reporting the information in the documents literally. I freed myself from his grip and ran headlong without looking back. Two bullets whistled through the air.

I didn't go back to my apartment, but I inquired about Hanna Yusif's new address—the coward had changed lodging. Someone I knew told me that he was living in a small place called Hotel Hamameh at the end of al-Rashid Street. When I arrived there I found it to be a miserable one-star hotel with a small reception hall and an aged Egyptian receptionist guarding a bunch of keys. Hanna was in room thirteen, on the second floor. I climbed the stairs, two steps at a time, ignoring the receptionist's protests, "Sir! If you please. Sir!"

I arrived in front of Hanna's room determined to enter without knocking, to force my way in if need be. The door was broken however, and I had no trouble opening it, and pulled off the door handle in the process. Hanna was just coming out of the restroom and buttoning his trousers, a cigarette between his lips. He could see in my eyes how upset and angry I was. He squeezed the cigarette between his teeth and said in a low voice, "How wonderful it is to be able to answer the call of nature, it is such a relief!" I jumped at him, grabbed him by his necktie, pushed him to the floor with my left hand, and fell onto him. He managed to wriggle out of my grasp like a louse, but I held him down by putting my knee on his belly and throttling him by the neck with my hand. I held my shoe in my other hand and whacked him on the head and face, "Son of a bitch, where's the money? I'll smash your head with this shoe"

He was pleading with me, his mouth foaming, lips turning blue, neck stiffening, eyes white. I hit him and threatened him further, "I'll kill you, you son of a bitch!" He smiled when he heard those words, then began laughing loudly and tried to free his neck. I couldn't understand why he was laughing as I was still threatening to pound him with my shoe. Unable to control himself, he said "I'm laughing at your curses. I have never heard those words before, *ibn al-'arida*."

I started laughing too and gradually released my grip. We sat on the floor and laughed. He jockeyed to gain the advantage, but I threatened again to kill him and said, "You won't walk through this door without paying me." He kept repeating, "I will, I will, just calm down." I repeated, "I won't calm down. You conned me, you didn't tell me that Ismail Hadoub was Sadeq Zadeh."

"I thought you knew," he said.

"How could I?" I said.

He found more excuses, "You're an intelligent man. You could have found out. You uncovered many secrets."

But I insisted, "What about the money? Are you trying to get out of paying me?" Finally, he told the truth, "I don't have the money." The blood rushed to my head.

I stood up and advised him, "I am going to cut off your nose and hand it over to you, do you understand? If you don't pay me right now, I'll stick each piece of furniture in this room up you know where." He chortled loudly. The arms holding his torso relaxed suddenly, and he jerked backward and hit his head on the floor. Hanna was pleading, "Oh, God, don't make me laugh. You're so funny. Just looking at you amuses me. When I hear those swear words I can't control myself."

I replied angrily, "My curses are not meant for your amusement, you rotten shoe. Do you understand?"

I searched his pockets for money. He helped me go through his clothes, showing me the secret pockets in his suit. There was nothing in them but a few Iraqi banknotes, two sexually explicit pictures, a small notebook, and a lighter. I noticed a small briefcase on the bed. I opened it and dumped out its contents: an old worn-out book, a fake Yves Saint Laurent perfume box, and a counterfeit identity card issued by Yaacub Saleh Yaacub's travel agency.

"Take this book as security until I bring you the money tomorrow at ten o'clock. Wait for me here at this hotel," said Hanna.

"Which book?" I asked.

"This book. It is an original manuscript that dates back to the tenth century." I examined the book and could see that its well-worn cover and its paper resembled old manuscripts, but I was still suspicious.

"You're lying, this is not an authentic ancient manuscript, it's a counterfeit."

He was adamant, "By Christ, it's not a counterfeit! Look, there's even the stamp of Hajji Khalifeh. I went to Father Anastas al-Karmali, and he helped me buy it from a priest who works in the convent I paid a very high price for it." I was not convinced and told him so but he swore again by Christ.

I finally said, "I'll break your neck if it's not authentic." He reconfirmed the time and the place to deliver my money, "I'll wait for you here tomorrow. You should know that no amount of money can compensate me for the value of this book, in case you decide to take it and ran away with it."

I defended myself. "I'm not a thief like you." His face expressed his disapproval.

I took the manuscript as Hanna was repacking his case. I left still wondering whether the manuscript was really worth the amount he had agreed to give me for writing the al-Sadriya philosopher's biography. I decided to confirm its authenticity before Hanna ran off completely. I went directly to the Iraqi Manuscript Center across the Tigris, an old house built in the thirties. It was a cold and windy day despite the shining sun. I knocked nervously at the door and waited for a few minutes, but no one came. I started banging very hard and shook the door, shouting loudly, "Open the door! Open the door."

Now I realized my mistake. In my haste to verify the authenticity of the manuscript, I had behaved in a way that made the people of the house suspicious. They looked at me distrustfully from an upper-floor window. I begged them to check the manuscript right away. Two guards took hold of me and led me inside. They snatched away the manuscript and passed it to a thin, graying man who looked like Pasteur. He examined it with the help of a magnifying glass and said, smiling, "It's a counterfeit."

I went back to the hotel immediately, but the Egyptian receptionist told me that Hanna had checked out. I looked for him everywhere but found no trace of him. A few days later I learned that he had gone to Jordan. He blackmailed Sadeq Zadeh with the manuscript he had taken from my apartment and received a significant sum of money. He was cooling his heels in Amman waiting for an immigration visa to

Canada. And that's where it all ended. I couldn't ask Sadeq Zadeh or Nunu Behar for money; my stupidities could have destroyed them.

All my efforts went to naught. I started looking for a job but soon realized that I was too lazy for any work that required physical effort. The only job that really suited me was writing. One day with a friend I went to a concert by the Iraqi National Symphony Orchestra at the Abbasid Palace overlooking the river. Men and women were dressed in their best clothes, and the place was bustling. It was a cosmopolitan crowd.

When my friend went to drink a cup of tea in the garden, I stood alone, leaning against a column and smoking. I felt a tap on my shoulder. It was Nunu Behar—a transformed Nunu wearing tight trousers and a long white chemise to her hips. She wore no makeup. I was a little concerned when she greeted me because I knew deep inside that Sadeq could never forgive me, and the documents that Hanna took from my apartment could well have destroyed him. He wouldn't believe me if I told him that Hanna had stolen them; he'd think that I had sold them to him for a tidy sum. He might even think that I had plotted with Hanna against him. Then I heard Nunu tell me that Michel wanted to see me. I was surprised and asked, admiring her beautiful face, "Michel? Who is Michel?"

"You don't know? I'll give you the address. We'll expect you tomorrow," she said coquettishly, smiling in her seductive manner. She searched in her purse and gave me a visiting card with the address. "We have a job for you, better than the other one. This time you'll make a lot of money."

The garden emptied of people, and the concert resumed. My friend returned and suggested we go back in. She looked in amazement at Nunu, mistaking her for a man. Nunu said to her, "We're old friends. I'll leave you now. We'll see you tomorrow. Don't be late. Michel is expecting you."

My friend asked me, "Who is he?" As the conductor raised the baton I replied, "I don't know anymore."

The following morning I went to the address listed on the card. It was in the Waziriya district. I crossed the British cemetery, entered Turkish Embassy Street, and came out right in front of an old house with a white fence and a brown-tiled roof. The garden was full of high trees and had a large iron gate. The servant led me into the living room. The place was tastefully furnished with a small piano and an aquarium. The walls were decorated with pastel Impressionist paintings, signed in English by Khuder Jerjis, an Iraqi painter. There were also two photographs, one of Sartre and one of Michel Foucault, one hand covering his mouth, the other on the back of an armchair.

"Welcome," said Nunu and led me by the hand to a small table near the window overlooking the garden. She had undergone a total change. Her hair was cut very short, like a boy's. She was wearing men's trousers and a large blouse that hid her big breasts, and she smoked a cigar. She offered me one but I told her that I smoked a different kind. She asked why, so I said, "This is a strong cigar, fit for a strong man like you." She laughed heartily then announced Michel's arrival.

To my surprise, Michel turned out to be the same Ismail Hadoub or Sadeq Zadeh. He had shaved his head completely and wore gold-framed glasses that resembled Foucault's. With his height, thin body, white shirt, shaven head, and foxy eyes he looked very much like the Foucault in the photograph on the wall. He greeted me in a philosophical manner and donned an inquisitive look, sat down, and placed one hand over his mouth and the other on the back of the armchair where Nunu was sitting. He was smiling while he looked me over. Nunu got down to business. "Michel has a huge project. You can make a lot of money from it and give Michel a chance to serve Arabic culture." I asked, my voice slightly choking, "What is this project?"

"A book," said Nunu.

Michel turned his shaven head in my direction; he looked like a cat considering a piece of red meat. He had lost his edginess, however, and spoke eloquently to impress me with his superior intellect. "I found Sartre useless for Arabic culture, as nihilism and nausea didn't manage to solve our problems, but I read Michel Foucault and discovered that structuralism is the one approach that will work for us. I want to write a book that explains this idea. What do you think?"

I was overcome with an oppressive feeling. I asked him with little interest, "I don't understand, who will write the book?"

"You," he said hesitantly, blushing.

Nunu intervened, "You'll get the money, and Michel will put his name on the book."

"He will put Michel Foucault's name on the cover?" I asked in an obviously sarcastic tone.

"No, he will use his new name, the Structuralist of Waziriya. After the death of the Existentialist of al-Sadriya, we have to invent a new philosopher for Baghdad, and this will be none other than the Structuralist of Waziriya," Nunu clarified. The new, would-be philosopher continued sitting in the same manner as the Foucault who hung on the wall.

"Well, what is that book? What kind of book?" I asked.

He explained, "You know that Foucault wrote a book about the madness of the classical period and used it to denounce western culture. We'd like a similar book in which you would denounce Arabic culture. We'll write a book about the madness of the Islamic period."

Before I could utter a single word, Nunu spoke up, "This time you'll get your money in installments."

The philosopher added in an accent that resembled that of a notable Iraqi man, "We'll give you the royalties we make from the book as well."

Lighting a cigarette, I interjected, "Well, we'll face a problem you may not have thought about." Nunu rushed to light my cigarette.

"What's that?" The philosopher asked.

"Who said that Islamic culture marginalizes madness? I don't think it does. A mad person has a respectable place in society, and the proof is you."

Both exploded in laughter, "Are you sure?" asked the philosopher, smiling.

"Do you have any doubt?" I asked.

Nunu chimed in, ready to light up another thick cigar, "Please, no mockery."

The philosopher approved, "Don't you see that Islamic philosophy did not marginalize madness and as a result fell victim to illogical thinking. Otherwise where in our culture could it have come from? It must have come to us from within our civilization, which did not marginalize madness as western culture did."

"Sound idea," I concurred, trying to avoid getting sucked into the project.

Michel explained, "All right. We'll write a book condemning Islamic civilization because it did not marginalize madness. Had reason prevailed in our civilization, madness would have been marginalized, and because madness has not been marginalized our civilization has became illogical."

"Great, great," shouted Nunu and almost sat on Michel's lap. He laughed loudly, stood up, clapped, and went to the bar. Nunu got up as well. They danced and swayed for joy, holding up their whiskey glasses and drinking to structuralism and the death of existentialism. This crazy man was dreaming of changing the viewpoint of the whole Arab population, from the Atlantic Ocean to the Arabian Gulf, by having them adopt structuralism. Men would shave their heads and wear gold-framed glasses. Women would cut their hair short like boys

and wear pants. I didn't know how to get out of my predica-
ment. I stood up and began dancing with them, drinking to the
health of the newborn structuralism. I was shouting, dancing,
and rocking back and forth. The chairs in the living room were
overturned, and the servants looked on in shock. When both
Nunu and Michel fell to the floor, I opened the door and ran as
fast as I could.

One day I was walking down the street and saw a black and
white stork land on the Turkish embassy. I crossed the street
under a soft sun. Traffic was moving smoothly, and I heard the
voices of the newspaper salesmen and cigarette merchants and
the car horns all around me. A man in white headgear was walking in front of me. He was holding a string of prayer beads, and
a woman wrapped totally in black walked behind him. Someone
shouted, "Sheikh Jamal, Sheikh Jamal." I don't know why, but
at this exact moment I thought of Jamal al-Din al-Afghani and
how Ismail Hadoub might have been influenced by him. Guided
by this philosopher he would likely be wearing a white turban
and holding prayer beads, while Nunu would be walking behind
him wrapped in black from head to toe.

Modern Arabic Literature
from the American University in Cairo Press

Ibrahim Abdel Meguid *Birds of Amber* • *Distant Train*
No One Sleeps in Alexandria • *The Other Place*
Yahya Taher Abdullah *The Collar and the Bracelet* • *The Mountain of Green Tea*
Leila Abouzeid *The Last Chapter*
Hamdi Abu Golayyel *A Dog with No Tail* • *Thieves in Retirement*
Yusuf Abu Rayya *Wedding Night*
Ahmed Alaidy *Being Abbas el Abd*
Idris Ali *Dongola* • *Poor*
Radwa Ashour *Granada*
Ibrahim Aslan *The Heron* • *Nile Sparrows*
Alaa Al Aswany *Chicago* • *Friendly Fire* • *The Yacoubian Building*
Fadhil al-Azzawi *Cell Block Five* • *The Last of the Angels*
Ali Bader *Papa Sartre*
Liana Badr *The Eye of the Mirror*
Hala El Badry *A Certain Woman* • *Muntaha*
Salwa Bakr *The Golden Chariot* • *The Man from Bashmour*
The Wiles of Men
Halim Barakat *The Crane*
Hoda Barakat *Disciples of Passion* • *The Tiller of Waters*
Mourid Barghouti *I Saw Ramallah*
Mohamed Berrada *Like a Summer Never to Be Repeated*
Mohamed El-Bisatie *Clamor of the Lake*
Houses Behind the Trees • *Hunger*
A Last Glass of Tea • *Over the Bridge*
Mahmoud Darwish *The Butterfly's Burden*
Tarek Eltayeb *Cities without Palms*
Mansoura Ez Eldin *Maryam's Maze*
Ibrahim Farghali *The Smiles of the Saints*
Hamdy el-Gazzar *Black Magic*
Fathy Ghanem *The Man Who Lost His Shadow*
Randa Ghazy *Dreaming of Palestine*
Gamal al-Ghitani *Pyramid Texts* • *The Zafarani Files* • *Zayni Barakat*
Tawfiq al-Hakim *The Essential Tawfiq al-Hakim*
Yahya Hakki *The Lamp of Umm Hashim*
Abdelilah Hamdouchi *The Final Bet*
Bensalem Himmich *The Polymath* • *The Theocrat*
Taha Hussein *The Days* • *A Man of Letters* • *The Sufferers*
Sonallah Ibrahim *Cairo: From Edge to Edge* • *The Committee* • *Zaat*
Yusuf Idris *City of Love and Ashes* • *The Essential Yusuf Idris*
Denys Johnson-Davies *The AUC Press Book of Modern Arabic Literature*
In a Fertile Desert: Modern Writing from the United Arab Emirates
Under the Naked Sky: Short Stories from the Arab World
Said al-Kafrawi *The Hill of Gypsies*

Sahar Khalifeh *The End of Spring*
The Image, the Icon, and the Covenant • *The Inheritance*
Edwar al-Kharrat *Rama and the Dragon* • *Stones of Bobello*
Betool Khedairi *Absent*
Mohammed Khudayyir *Basrayatha*
Ibrahim al-Koni *Anubis* • *Gold Dust* • *The Seven Veils of Seth*
Naguib Mahfouz *Adrift on the Nile* • *Akhenaten: Dweller in Truth*
Arabian Nights and Days • *Autumn Quail* • *Before the Throne* • *The Beggar*
The Beginning and the End • *Cairo Modern*
The Cairo Trilogy: Palace Walk, Palace of Desire, Sugar Street
Children of the Alley • *The Day the Leader Was Killed*
The Dreams • *Dreams of Departure* • *Echoes of an Autobiography*
The Harafish • *The Journey of Ibn Fattouma* • *Karnak Café*
Khan al-Khalili • *Khufu's Wisdom* • *Life's Wisdom* • *Midaq Alley*
The Mirage • *Miramar* • *Mirrors* • *Morning and Evening Talk*
Naguib Mahfouz at Sidi Gaber • *Respected Sir* • *Rhadopis of Nubia*
The Search • *The Seventh Heaven* • *Thebes at War*
The Thief and the Dogs • *The Time and the Place*
Voices from the Other World • *Wedding Song*
Mohamed Makhzangi *Memories of a Meltdown*
Alia Mamdouh *The Loved Ones* • *Naphtalene*
Selim Matar *The Woman of the Flask*
Ibrahim al-Mazini *Ten Again*
Yousef Al-Mohaimeed *Wolves of the Crescent Moon*
Ahlam Mosteghanemi *Chaos of the Senses* • *Memory in the Flesh*
Shakir Mustafa *Contemporary Iraqi Fiction: An Anthology*
Mohamed Mustagab *Tales from Dayrut*
Buthaina Al Nasiri *Final Night*
Ibrahim Nasrallah *Inside the Night*
Haggag Hassan Oddoul *Nights of Musk*
Mohamed Mansi Qandil *Moon over Samarqand*
Abd al-Hakim Qasim *Rites of Assent*
Somaya Ramadan *Leaves of Narcissus*
Lenin El-Ramly *In Plain Arabic*
Mekkawi Said *Cairo Swan Song*
Ghada Samman *The Night of the First Billion*
Mahdi Issa al-Saqr *East Winds, West Winds*
Rafik Schami *Damascus Nights* • *The Dark Side of Love*
Khairy Shalaby *The Lodging House*
Miral al-Tahawy *Blue Aubergine* • *Gazelle Tracks* • *The Tent*
Bahaa Taher *As Doha Said* • *Love in Exile*
Fuad al-Takarli *The Long Way Back*
Zakaria Tamer *The Hedgehog*
M.M. Tawfik *Murder in the Tower of Happiness*
Mahmoud Al-Wardani *Heads Ripe for Plucking*
Latifa al-Zayyat *The Open Door*